Sir Greydon Varleigh was undoubtedly one of the Season's most eligible bachelors. A Corinthian, dashing, dark and handsome, there was many a designing mama who had her eyes on him. But Sir Greydon was reluctant to marry. It was only when he promised his ageing grandmama that he would find a bride before the year was out that he realised he would probably have to settle for one of the Season's vapid young debutantes.

It was unfortunate that the only woman who took his fancy was the impoverished, outspoken, not particularly pretty daughter of crumbling Garth House...

Also in the Georgian Romance Series

THE GEORGIAN RAKE by Alice Chetwynd Ley
THE JEWELLED SNUFFBOX by Alice Chetwynd Ley
THE SCAPEGRACE by Sylvia Thorpe
THE RELUCTANT ADVENTURESS by Sylvia Thorpe
THE SMUGGLER'S BRIDE by Rosalind Laker
ROMANTIC LADY by Sylvia Thorpe
TARRINGTON CHASE by Sylvia Thorpe
THE SILVER NIGHTINGALE by Sylvia Thorpe
A SPEAKING LIKENESS by Sheila Bishop
THE SWYNDEN NECKLACE by Mira Stables
THE BEAU AND THE BLUESTOCKING by Alice Chetwynd Ley
ROGUE'S COVENANT by Sylvia Thorpe
THE SCANDALOUS LADY ROBIN by Sylvia Thorpe
HONEY-POT by Mira Stables
THE MARRIAGE MART by Patricia Burns

and published by Corgi Books

SYLVIA THORPE

THE VARLEIGH MEDALLION

CORGI BOOKS

A DIVISION OF TRANSWORLD PUBLISHERS LTD

THE VARLEIGH MEDALLION

A CORGI BOOK 0 552 11253 4

Originally published in Great Britain by
Hurst & Blackett Ltd.

PRINTING HISTORY
Hurst & Blackett edition published 1979
Corgi edition published 1980

Corgi Books are published by
Transworld Publishers Ltd.,
Century House, 61–63 Uxbridge Road,
Ealing, London W5 5SA

Printed in the United States by
Offset Paperbacks Inc., Dallas, Pa.

THE VARLEIGH MEDALLION

Part I

The 'Royal George' was a posting-house, and though by no means as large or as well known as the famous inns of the great highways, it was, as its owner, Mr Henry Hobkin, was fond of asserting, an establishment of the highest order. It catered almost exclusively for the Quality and though if some prosperous tradesman chanced to break his journey there his wants were civilly attended to, it was made plain to him in subtle ways that this was by favour and not by right.

It was therefore with a sensation of mild outrage that, on a chilly, overcast evening in May, Mr Hobkin beheld two unescorted and shabbily dressed young women enter the inn-yard on foot from the street outside. From the window of the temporarily deserted coffee-room he watched them approach, the taller of the two walking purposefully and her companion following with obvious reluctance. Moving to listen at the door giving on to the passage, he was able to discover that they wished to hire a carriage, and he nodded silent approval of the civil but very definite refusal of the request by the passing waiter to whom it was addressed. That should have been the end of the matter, but the spokeswoman of the pair was unexpectedly persistent and the waiter, who was young and inexperienced, began to sound harassed. Mr Hobkin heaved a sigh of exasperation and went himself to send these unwanted guests about their business.

Miss Dione Mallory, seeing him emerge into the passage and wave dismissal to the waiter, braced herself for battle. She was no stranger to the disagreeable consequences of being poor, having lived with them for the whole of her twenty-two years, but she had never learned to like them. However, since it had fallen to her to fend not only for herself but also for the rest of the family, she was resigned to the sort of humiliation now confronting her, and only very occasionally reflected wistfully how pleasant it would be to have such battles fought for her. Now, with the wisdom of experience, she gave Mr Hobkin no chance to speak, but said briskly:

'Are you the landlord? Excellent! I wish to hire a carriage to drive to Brambledon, and this man tells me that he cannot arrange it. Will *you* be good enough to see to it, if you please?'

Mr Hobkin bridled. It was bad enough to be expected to perform so menial task himself, but it was an added insult that this be demanded of him by a young person who had undoubtedly alighted only a short time ago from the common stage-coach which had halted at the 'Griffin' farther along the street. He said austerely:

'You have been correctly informed, miss. It cannot be arranged.'

'Why not? This is a posting-house, is it not?' Dione saw the way he was eyeing her, and added bluntly: 'Are you afraid we shall be unable to pay the charges? You need have no apprehension on that score.'

'Dee!' The younger girl, a very pretty, fragile-looking blonde, uttered an embarrassed protest which was not attended to, Miss Mallory merely saying practically:

'Well, I can perceive no other reason for him to refuse us. In fact,' she added, turning again to the innkeeper, 'I believe it is unlawful for you to do so. In any event, a carriage I must have, and there appears to be nowhere else where I may obtain one.'

Mr Hobkin glared at her. From the corner of his eye he

had detected a smirk on the departing waiter's face; there were sounds from the yard indicating that a carriage had just arrived there; a moment later he heard a voice he recognized as that of one of his most valued patrons. Clearly this tiresome young woman must be got rid of without delay.

'The landlord of the "Griffin" has a gig he lets out for hire,' he informed her tartly. 'You'd best ask him, miss, for I can't oblige you.'

'A gig is not the least use,' she began, but even as she spoke Mr Hobkin was brushing past her to greet a gentleman who had just entered, and Mr Hobkin's manner had undergone a rapid and remarkable change.

'Good evening, Sir Greydon.' He was bowing now and smiling, all affability. 'This is indeed an honour, sir! How may I serve you?'

The newcomer nodded an acknowledgement of the greeting, but shot a quick glance past the innkeeper towards the two young women. He said pleasantly:

'In no way, Hobkin, that cannot wait until you have attended to these ladies.'

'Thank you.' Miss Mallory, far from retreating in confusion as Mr Hobkin had hoped, came forward with what he could only regard as shocking boldness. 'I am merely endeavouring to hire a carriage, but so far have met with no success.'

Sir Greydon's brows lifted, and he cast a perceptive glance at the fuming Mr Hobkin. 'A reasonable request, one would suppose. What appears to be the difficulty?'

'I have already told the lady, sir, that she can hire a gig at the "Griffin"—!'

'And *I* have told *you* that a gig is not the least use, for we are traveling with our mama and our little brother and sister. We left London very early this morning, the stage could take us no nearer to our destination than this, and so a carriage we must have.'

To the indignant Mr Hobkin this merely sounded impertinent and overbearing, but the other man was more perceptive, and detected a faint undertone of desperation in her voice. It was no concern of his, but

Hobkin's sycophantic manner had irritated him for years, and he saw no reason why he should not exert a little of the influence he knew he possessed.

'A very natural desire, ma'am,' he agreed, and glanced at the innkeeper. 'Hobkin, you will oblige me by having the carriage these ladies require brought to the door as speedily as may be.'

It was pleasantly said, but unmistakably a command, and Mr Hobkin visibly changed colour. Swallowing his chagrin, he made haste to obey, and as he passed out of earshot, Sir Greydon, with a humorous glance at the young ladies, added confidentially:

'He is a shocking toadeater, of course; I have known him for years, so you must forgive me for puffing off my consequence a little.'

The younger sister blushed, and cast down her eyes, but the elder was betrayed into a little spurt of appreciative laughter.

'We forgive you freely, sir, for we stand very much in your debt, and must thank you for coming to our aid.'

'It was a pleasure, ma'am. You will not be kept waiting for long, but there is no need for you to stand in this draughty passage.' He stepped past them and opened a door. 'You will be more comfortable in the coffee-room.'

She inclined her head and moved forward, but her sister clutched her by the arm.

'Dee, we should not! I am sure Mama would say—!'

'Oh, come, love, what harm is there in going into a public room? See, there is no one here, and we may sit down and be comfortable for a few minutes, which I, at least, shall be heartily glad of after being jolted all day in that odiously uncomfortable coach. I am sure it is no wonder that poor little Theo feels so sadly out of sorts.'

She walked forward and disposed herself in a chair near the fireplace, and after a moment's hesitation, and a doubtful, timid glance at Sir Greydon, her sister fluttered after her and sat down close by. Sir Greydon himself followed them into the room, but remained standing by the open door.

'I fear, sir,' Miss Mallory observed politely after a few

minutes, 'that your kindness in helping us has led to your own requirements being neglected. I would have expected the innkeeper to send someone to attend to them.'

'It is of no consequence, I assure you,' he replied with a smile. 'I expect he means to teach me a lesson.'

Dione chuckled again, and looked consideringly at him, speculating upon his identity, for the innkeeper's attitude had made it plain that he was a person of some importance in the neighbourhood. He was clearly a man of fashion, yet there was nothing of the dandy about him, for he affected none of the more absurd extremes of attire, while his height and powerful build suggested the athlete rather than the drawing room beau. He was very dark, black-haired, and of a swarthiness of complexion startlingly emphasized by the snowy folds of an intricately arranged neckcloth, and though not handsome, his countenance compelled attention by a striking quality which had nothing to do with mere good looks. With characteristic decision Miss Mallory decided that she liked him, not least for the fact that there was no hint of gallantry in his manner. She feared none on her own account, but knew only too well that her shy, pretty sister could all too easily become the object of unwelcome attentions.

Sir Greydon was aware of her frank, appraising regard, and amused by it. He found it a novel experience to be so candidly assessed, for the young ladies he met were usually thrown into a confusion, either real or assumed, which manifested itself in blushes and flutterings and similarly missish behaviour which, had they but known it, bored him to distraction. This girl, with the expressive grey eyes and delightful chuckle, was regarding him as levelly as a man might have done; there was, in fact, a certain boyish directness about her, as though she had no patience with the more obvious feminine wiles and blandishments. No patience, or too strong a sense of humour.

'Have you much farther to travel, ma'am?' he enquired after a moment.

'A few miles only, sir, I believe. We are going to a village called Brambledon. Perhaps you know of it?'

He was surprised, for this was the village nearest to his own home, and he could not imagine for which household there the numerous family she had mentioned could be bound. It was obvious that she and her sister were gentle-women; it was equally obvious, from their shabby appearance and the reference to the stage-coach, that they were in straitened circumstances. Passing his neighbours under swift mental review, he had to admit himself at a loss, and was aware of a curiosity which it would be ill-bred to indulge.

'I do know it, ma'am,' he replied, 'and am able to tell you that you have a little less than six miles to go. You should reach Brambledon before dark.'

'Thank heaven for that!' she said fervently. 'I will confess, sir, that I had begun to wonder what was to become of us, until you were kind enough to use your good offices on our behalf. Believe me, I am very grateful.'

He smiled and shook his head, and there was silence until, a few minutes later, Mr Hobkin returned to inform them, with an ill-used air, that the carriage was at the door. Dione got up and turned to take leave of Sir Greydon, but he, having perceived an unexceptionable way to satisfy his curiosity, said easily:

'Permit me, ladies, to escort you to the carriage.'

He did so, and having handed the younger sister up into it, paused before performing a like service for the elder to inquire:

'Where, precisely, may I direct the post-boy to convey you, ma'am?'

'To the "Griffin" first, if you please, where Mama and the children are waiting, and then to Brambledon. To Garth House.'

She was looking up at him as she spoke, and was disconcerted to see a look of blank astonishment, almost of disbelief, cross his face. He seemed to be on the point of making some comment, then, as though thinking better of it, merely bowed, assisted her into the carriage, and turned to convey her directions to the post-boy. The steps were put up, the door closed, and the carriage jolted forward across the cobblestones.

As they passed under the archway and turned left-handed along the street, the younger Miss Mallory broke her long silence.

'Dee, how could you? To enter into conversation with a strange gentleman met at an inn! I was ready to sink.'

'I know you were, love, but it would have been the height of bad manners to sit mumchance, as though he were not there, when he had been of such help. That odious innkeeper would never have hired us a carriage if *he* had not insisted upon it.

'Yes, but what must he have thought? So fashionable, plainly accustomed to moving in the first circles—and you chatted with him as though you had been acquainted for years! It would be no wonder if he thought you dreadfully fast. You know, Dee, there are times when I blush for you.'

'Yes, Cecy, and I am very grateful to you,' Dione assured her earnestly, 'for you know how hard I find it to blush for myself.'

'Dee!' Cecilia was won to reluctant laughter. 'You are the most shocking creature! What Mama would say I cannot imagine.'

'I can,' her sister retorted rather wryly. 'I think we will make no mention of—what did the innkeeper call him? Sir Greydon! Or of the assistance he rendered us.'

'Greydon is a most uncommon name,' Cecilia remarked. 'I do not think I have heard it before.'

'No, nor I. Probably a family name. I wonder what the rest of it may be?'

'The innkeeper was known to him,' Cecilia offered, 'and he said himself that he knew Brambledon. Perhaps we shall find that we are neighbours.'

'Yes, perhaps.' Dione found that she did not wish to pursue that train of thought, for it recalled Sir Greydon's reaction when she told him their destination. He had looked—what? Startled? Shocked? What had he been about to say, and then changed his mind? He knew

Brambledon; what did he know of Garth House, to make him look so oddly at her when she spoke of it?

* * *

There proved to be no need for the girls to practise any deception upon their mother with regard to Sir Greydon, for she was too thankful to learn that they had succeeded in hiring a carriage to query the means by which this had been accomplished. They found her sitting between her two youngest children on a settle in the coffee-room at the 'Griffin', her arm around eleven-year-old Theodore, whose head rested on her shoulder. He was a delicate-looking little boy with the same fragile, blond good looks as his mother and second sister, and though even his fond mama would have been willing to admit that he was by no means as angelic as his appearance suggested, no one could deny that he was far from robust. The motion of the stuffy, overcrowded coach had made him violently ill, so that by the time the present stage of their journey was reached he was utterly worn out, and though the landlady of the 'Griffin', a kindly soul, had done all she could, he was still sufficiently exhausted seriously to alarm his mother. The health of her youngest child, the longed-for son whom his sailor father had not lived to see, was a constant source of anxiety to Mrs Mallory, and though she loved her daughters, Theodore's wellbeing was always her first concern.

It was primarily for Theodore's sake that the family were making this long, uncomfortable journey to an almost unknown destination, though as the day progressed Mrs Mallory's original misgivings had grown stronger and stronger. She was obliged to keep reminding herself that Dione felt certain it was the right thing to do; had insisted so strongly upon it that Mrs Mallory had finally been prevailed upon to follow a course of action which at first she had refused even to contemplate. Being of a gentle and pliable nature she had, over the years, come to depend completely upon her capable, practical eldest daughter, just as in the early days of her marriage she had depended upon her husband, whom Dione now greatly resembled.

Dione herself, looking at her little brother's white, exhausted face and closed eyes, was conscious of a stab of anxiety which was somehow an extension of the little nagging doubt of her own judgement that had been plaguing her ever since she observed Sir Greydon's curious reaction to the mention of Garth House. She dissembled this, however, saying with firm kindness:

'Come, Theo love, I have a carriage waiting. We shall soon be at our new home, and then you can be comfortable.'

He burrowed his head closer against his mother's shoulder, protesting fretfully that the jolting of the coach would make him sick again. Dione said patiently:

'It is not a coach this time, but a post-chaise, so we shall be travelling in prime style. Besides, we have less than six miles to go. Come along, love! Mama is tired, too, you know.'

He still protested, but allowed her to help him up and lead him out to the carriage. Mrs Mallory followed with Cecilia, while Edwina, who at fourteen not only looked very much like Dione but bade fair to become just as capable, gathered up various small items of baggage. Eventually they were all crammed into the chaise, the luggage was piled on the roof, and they were able to set out on the last stage of their journey.

As there was so little room, and Theodore was small and light for his age, Dione took him on her lap. For a time he was silent, but then, apparently finding that his worst fears were not to be realized, he revived sufficiently to say plaintively:

'Mama, tell me again what Garth House is like.'

Mrs Mallory, who had begun to doze fitfully in her corner of the chaise, roused herself with a start. 'My love, I have told you a dozen times already.'

'I know, but I want to hear it again. Please, Mama!'

She sighed, but as his wishes always came first with her she complied, the three girls listening resignedly to the now familiar recital.

'Well, dearest, you know that I have only visited Garth House once, and that was nearly twenty-five years ago, with dear Papa. It was just after we were married, and he took me to visit his cousin, Mr Jonathan Mallory. They were the only members of the family left, for Mr Jonathan had never married.

'It was early summer when we went, and I remember how very pretty the gardens were, with the roses just coming into bloom. There is a walled rose-garden, with flagged paths and a fountain in the centre. The house stands at the foot of a hill and is hidden from the road by a spinney through which the drive winds, and one supposes that it must be quite buried among trees, but it is not so at all. There is open space all around it, and a pool—almost a small lake—close by. The house itself is very old, with panelled rooms, and stone-flagged floors downstairs, and curious little corners and staircases.'

'Not a bit like Aunt Winton's house in London,' Theodore observed with deep satisfaction, 'and there is a stream, is there not, Mama?'

'Yes, my love, the stream that feeds the pool flows down through the woods behind the house in little waterfalls and cascades.'

'And it belongs to us? It is really our own?'

'It belongs to you, my dear son. You inherited it when Mr Jonathan Mallory died.'

Dione, who had been paying little attention to the conversation, at this point lost interest in it altogether and allowed her thoughts to wander, remembering the astonishment they had all felt when they learned of Theodore's inheritance. The news had not reached them until some ten months after old Jonathan Mallory's death, for the family tie between the two cousins had not been strong, and after her husband died Mrs Mallory had lost touch with his surviving kinsman, yet when the information finally reached them it seemed to Dione like a sign from Providence.

At that time the family were living in London with Mrs Mallory's elder sister. Amelia Winton was now also a widow, but there the similarity ended, for Amelia's husband had left her amply provided for. True, he had been what fashionable people contemptuously termed a Cit, for the Winton fortune had been made in banking, and Amelia's stepson, Eustace Winton, was still engaged in that line of business. Amelia, in fact, was felt to have married beneath her, but if this ever troubled her she was always able to console herself with her large house, her carriages and horses and fine clothes. Not for her the financial difficulties experienced by her younger sister as the wife, and then the widow, of an impecunious naval officer, struggling to bring up a growing family on an inadequate income.

Mrs Winton had always been generous to her less fortunate relations, but since this generosity went hand in hand with a desire to organize their lives, Dione had always faintly resented it. Then Mr Winton died, and Aunt Amelia announced that since she had no children of her own and her stepdaughters were married, she was in need of company and they must come to live with her. Eustace Winton was quite happy with the proposed arrangement, but Dione, then seventeen and already of independent spirit, was only won over by her mother's plea that it would be better for Theodore. She could not like it, but there was no denying that the delicate little boy would enjoy in his aunt's house a greater degree of care and cosseting than even the most loving mother and sisters could provide in their hand-to-mouth existence.

Yet Theodore had not thrived as they had hoped. The heat and dust of London summers drained him of strength, while winter fogs left him with a racking cough; that April he had been frighteningly frail after a really serious illness, and the doctor had told Mrs Mallory bluntly that what the boy needed was country air. He would never be well while he lived in the city.

Barely a week later had come the lawyer's letter informing Mrs Mallory of old Jonathan's death, and that the property of Garth House now belonged to her son. When the first astonishment had subsided, and Mrs Mallory, drawing upon her almost forgotten memories of the place, had described it to them, Dione was seized by what seemed to her an inspiration. Why, she suggested, did they not go to live at Garth House?

The suggestion was not well received. Mrs Mallory, after five years in her sister's household, shrank from the responsibility of an establishment of her own; Mrs Winton, outraged and reproachful by turns, declared that her niece must be out of her mind; Eustace said gravely that he could not agree to his aunt and cousins living alone in a strange place with no man to advise and protect them. He would, he said, find a reliable tenant for Garth House for the next ten years, which would help to pay for Theodore's education, then, when the boy came of age, he could decide for himself what he wished to do with the property.

Eustace, however, had his own reasons for wishing his cousins to stay in London. For more than a year he had been trying to persuade Dione to marry him, but though during that time he had won the support of the other adult members of the family, Dione herself remained adamant. Mrs Winton was particularly anxious for the match, the mercenary streak which had prompted her own marriage making her eager to keep the Winton wealth in the family. Mrs Mallory said that Dee was old enough to make her own decision, but as time went by and Mrs Winton constantly urged upon her all the advantages of such a marriage, she said it less and less frequently. Even Cecilia made no secret of the fact that she felt Dee ought to be guided by duty rather than inclination.

Which was all very well for Cecy, Dione reflected now, shifting Theodore's weight a little to ease her cramped arms. She was gentle and biddable, always willing to have decisions made for her, which Dione herself was not. She was not a person of strong emotions, never even fancying herself in love with the young men who from time to time expressed an admiration for her, but rather being alarmed by such declarations. Dione had never been in love, either, and did not expect to be, but she knew that to enter into the married state she would need to feel something warmer for her bridegroom than the mixture of tolerance, exasperation and somewhat resentful gratitude which was the sum total of her feelings where Eustace was concerned. The thought of committing herself to him for the rest of her life was something she could not face, for he was a domestic tyrant, self-opinionated and totally lacking in humour.

Yet she could appreciate the impossible situation which would arise if she continued to live in his house and did not accept his proposal—sometimes she even feared that that circumstance alone might force her into an unwelcome marriage. Garth House had offered a heaven-sent means of escape, and she had taken it as much for her own sake as for Theodore's, winning her mother's slightly bemused assent with the force of her own enthusiasm, and not hesitating to quarrel so violently with her aunt that Mrs Winton flatly refused to advance money for the journey, which was why they had been obliged to travel uncomfortably by stage-coach. Eustace was as yet unaware of their departure. A matter of business had taken him to the north, and Dione had seized the opportunity of avoiding further argument by leaving London while he was away.

Her thoughts darted ahead to the new home waiting for them now so close at hand. A home which was really their own, something they had never had in their lives. The bulk of old Mr Mallory's income had apparently died with him, for Garth House brought with it only a meagre sum, but that, together with their own modest means, should enable them to live in some degree of comfort. They ought to be largely self-supporting, for Mrs Mallory's recollections of the property included kitchen-garden and orchard and poultry-yard. Dione knew herself to be an efficient and provident housekeeper, and though they might lack some of the luxuries they had enjoyed at the Winton house, she felt sure they would go on prosperously enough.

She had almost succeeded in quieting her recent doubts and recovering the mood of happy optimism in which she had set out that morning when there was the sound of another vehicle coming up fast behind them, and a few moments later a curricle dashed past. Dione had a fleeting impression of four perfectly matched black horses, of a groom sitting statue-like with folded arms, of a tall driver in a many-caped coat, hands steady on the reins, his profile dark and unmistakable below the rakish brim of a tall beaver hat. Theodore, who was passionately interested in horses, exclaimed and sat upright, peering eagerly after the sporting carriage, but Dione made no response; all her misgivings had sprung to life again, revived by that brief glimpse of Sir Greydon and the memory of the blank disbelief in his eyes when he learned where they were bound.

It was dusk by the time the chaise turned from the road along a drive which, as Mrs Mallory had described, wound upwards to the lower slopes of the hill looming on their left. It was nearly dark beneath the trees, for the spinney of twenty-five years before had become a wood, and the chaise lurched along at a snail's pace over bumps and ruts, while branches scraped the luggage on the roof and even brushed against the windows. A somewhat uneasy silence descended on the occupants of the carriage, and Dione, with increasing disquiet, thought again of Sir Greydon. At last the drive levelled out, and they emerged from the shadows of the wood; gravel crunched beneath the wheels and the chaise came to a halt. There was a pause, and then the post-boy opened the door and let down the steps. Theodore, revived by curiosity, slid from his sister's lap and scrambled out. Dione followed, and then froze into stillness, staring about her, riveted by shock.

* * *

Before her loomed a tall old house, timbered, as her mother had said, with a many-gabled roof and diamond-paned windows. A vast wisteria, its lower stems as thick as tree-trunks, writhed and sprawled across it, smothering the façade in a mass of leaves and pendant blossoms which overhung windows where more than one pane showed cracked or broken, and encroached even upon the great, iron-studded door. The gravel beneath her feet was thick with weeds, and the gardens a tangle of greenery where wild flowers and cultivated flourished together. To her right, the pool sullenly reflected the last of the light, while the unseasonably chilly wind sighed through the reeds surrounding it and ruffled the surface of the water. No glimmer of light showed at any window, nor was there the least sound to suggest that the house was inhabited, and in the gathering darkness it seemed hostile and almost sinister, resenting their intrusion.

For one incredulous moment Dione thought that the post-boy had made a mistake and brought them to the wrong place, but even as the thought formed in her mind she realized how closely in some respects this resembled her mother's description of Garth House. The only mistake, she thought wretchedly, was her own, in committing them all irrevocably to this mad venture.

The post-boy, who had been staring about him open-mouthed, said blankly: 'Be you expected, miss? Don't seem to be no one here.'

'There must be!' Dione tried to speak calmly, but was aware that rising panic sounded in her voice. She swallowed hard, and drew a deep breath before going on. 'There are servants—a housekeeper and her husband and daughter. I wrote to tell her we were coming. Will you be good enough to knock upon the door?'

He looked doubtful, but went up the two shallow steps and beat a resounding tattoo with the heavy iron knocker. The sound woke an echo from the far side of the pool and reverberated hollowly within the house, but there was no response. Mrs Mallory, following her other two daughters from the chaise, looked about her in a dazed fashion.

'Oh!' she said faintly. 'Oh, heaven preserve us! Dee, what have we *done*?' She burst into tears.

'It does not look quite as you told us, Mama,' Theodore said doubtfully, 'but never mind. It is my house, and *I* like it.'

'Pray do not cry, Mama.' Dione put her arm round her

mother's thin shoulders, trying to dissemble her own dismay. 'The house is neglected, of course, but—!'

'Neglected?' Mrs Mallory was searching in her reticule for her handkerchief; her voice rose hysterically. 'It must have been going to rack and ruin for years! We should not have come! Eustace was right—gentlemen always know best in such matters—but you are so *headstrong*, Dee—!'

'Hush, love!' Dione was acutely aware that the post-boy, having ceased his assault upon the knocker, was listening with deep interest to this exchange. She addressed him with some asperity. 'Knock again, if you please.'

He did so, though with an ill grace. As the echoes died away, Theodore said excitedly:

'Look! Someone is coming.'

A light was glimmering faintly behind the grimy panes of the tall windows flanking the door. There was the sound of rusty bolts being drawn and the door opened a few inches to reveal a masculine figure, holding a single candle and peering suspiciously through the narrow aperture, for the door was still secured by a substantial chain.

'Who be there?' demanded a surly voice.

Quite suddenly Dione began to grow angry. No matter what state of decay Garth House had fallen into, or how inadequate the resources upon which the late Mr Mallory's servants had to depend, there was no excuse for conduct of this kind. Resigning her place at her mother's side to Cecilia, she went briskly up the steps, saying sharply:

'It is Mrs Mallory. You were informed that we should be arriving this evening, so there is no need to behave as though the house were under siege. Open the door immediately!'

After an instant of stunned silence the command was obeyed, and the door opened with a shriek of rusty hinges. Dione, wincing at the discordant sound, added in the same brisk voice:

'First thing tomorrow, be good enough to grease those

hinges. We cannot have that noise every time the door is opened.' She then turned, holding out a hand to her brother and saying in a rallying tone: 'Come, Theo! You are the master of the house, you know.'

He came promptly, looking about him with eager curiosity, while Mrs Mallory and the girls followed with less enthusiasm. Dione shepherded them all past her into the hall, and then turned to survey the man who had admitted them.

His appearance matched his surroundings. He was middle-aged and slightly stooping, with a morose expression and an untidy thatch of iron grey hair, and was dressed in a livery coat of some indeterminate colour, greasy and threadbare and incongruously mated with thick frieze breeches, much darned stockings and clumsy shoes; his linen was by no means clean. The feeble light of the candle he held did little to enhance his appearance, and nothing at all to dispel the gloom of their surroundings.

'You, I collect, are John Ibstone?' Dione inquired, and received a grunt of assent. 'I am Miss Mallory. Pray be good enough to light some more candles, and then fetch Mrs Ibstone. After that you may help the post-boy with the baggage.'

Mr Ibstone looked as though he would have liked to argue, but was daunted by the self-possession of the young lady confronting him. He muttered something under his breath, but used his candle to light three others in a candelabrum on a massive table in the middle of the room and then slouched off towards the back of the house.

Dione picked up the light and held it aloft so that they could see something of their surroundings. They were standing in a large, stone-flagged hall panelled with age-blackened oak, with a staircase of the same dark wood rising in short, right-angled flights in one corner to serve a gallery across the far end of the room; a huge, stone-arched fireplace gaping midway along another wall was choked with the ashes of long-dead fires; the whole place was thick with dust, musty with the smell of mice and decay, and draped everywhere with cobwebs.

'They might at least have swept the floor,' Edwina said flatly.

'They might indeed,' Dione agreed. 'It appears to me that no preparations at all have been made for us.' She put down the candles and turned to her mother, who, regardless of the dust, had sunk into the nearest chair and was weeping quietly into her handkerchief. 'Mama dear, this has been a horrid shock for you, and everything seems quite dreadful, but it will look differently in the morning, I promise you.'

'It is my fault!' Mrs Mallory lifted a ravaged, tear-streaked face. 'If I had not described Garth House as I did you would never have thought of removing here. But it *was* like that, Dee! A charming place, just as I told you.'

'Twenty-five years ago!' Dione said wryly. 'You must not blame yourself, Mama. You were not to know that everything has changed here.'

'We shall have to make the best of it,' Mrs Mallory said woefully, wiping her eyes. 'At least we have a roof over our heads, and that is something to be thankful for, I suppose.'

From the general appearance of Garth House, Dione felt that it might be unwise to place too much dependence on the roof in question, but she refrained from saying so. Footsteps were approaching from the back of the house, and she turned to confront the housekeeper.

Mrs Ibstone was enormously fat. Her rusty black gown was strained across a vast bosom, she wheezed from the effort of walking from the kitchen, and her broad face was florid and shiny, framed by untidy grey curls beneath a limp and grubby cap. She came clearly prepared to do battle, her hands folded across a wide expanse of greasy apron, her mouth small and hard in the fleshy folds of her face, though her belligerence wilted a little before the cool, critical regard of Miss Mallory's expressive grey eyes.

'Good evening, Mrs Ibstone.' Dione spoke pleasantly though with some firmness. 'Did you not receive my letter telling you that we would arrive this evening?'

'Not till this morning.' The housekeeper saw Miss Mallory's brow lift, and added grudgingly: 'Ma'am.'

Dione glanced round the hall. 'You do not appear to have acted upon it.'

'We've took our orders from Mr Birkett ever since the master died.' There was insolence in the woman's voice. 'He never said nothing about anyone coming to live here.'

Birkett was Jonathan Mallory's lawyer, and lived in the little market town where they had alighted from the stagecoach. When he had written to Mrs Mallory to tell her of Theodore's inheritance, Dione had replied on her mother's behalf, but there had seemed no need to inform him in advance of their intention to remove to Garth House.

'Mr Birkett must have told you that the house now belongs to my brother,' Dione said sharply, for she had no intention of being browbeaten by Mrs Ibstone. 'However, there is no time to go into that now, for if nothing has been made ready to receive us, there is a great deal to do. Wait a moment while I settle with the post-boy.'

As she turned towards the door again she saw the woman exchange a glance with her husband, who had followed her back to the hall and was now hovering indecisively nearby. Dione received a distinct impression of their mutual surprise and dismay, and knew, as surely as though it had been put into words, that her letter had been deliberately ignored in the hope that one look at the state of the house would be enough to send them away again in search of more comfortable quarters at an inn. As it might well have done, she reflected ruefully, if they had possessed sufficient funds.

Having paid off the post-boy and seen him, grudgingly assisted by Ibstone, begin to carry the baggage into the house, Dione returned to join issue with the housekeeper, who would, she fancied, prove a more formidable opponent than her husband. Mrs Ibstone had not moved. She still stood with folded hands, positively radiating hostility, while Mrs Mallory drooped in her chair with Theodore, his brief excitement spent, leaning wearily against her and the other two girls standing close beside them. The little family group seemed intimidated by the housekeeper's baleful presence, and Dione felt her anger bubbling again.

'Now, Mrs Ibstone,' she said briskly, 'we cannot sit here in the hall, so, first, please be good enough to show us where we may be more comfortable. Wherever it was that Mr Mallory used to sit, perhaps.'

The woman looked resentfully at her for a moment, found that she could not stare her down, and reluctantly picked up the candles. Dione helped her mother to her feet, took Theodore by the hand, and with her sisters trailing after them followed the housekeeper towards a door at the rear of the hall.

This proved to lead to the parlour, a square, low-pitched room which might have been pleasant had it been less dusty and dilapidated. The window was long and low, with a broad seat below it, and the fireplace, though framed by an arch of stone like the one in the hall, was much smaller and looked less like the gaping mouth of a cave. A high-backed chair piled with worn cushions stood beside it, into which Mrs Mallory sank with a sigh of relief, while a long table was pushed back against one wall to make room for one or two smaller chairs and a couple of stools. All the furniture was of heavily carved oak, and looked, Dione thought, as though it had been selected when the house was built and scarcely altered or added to since, but the parlour was appreciably warmer than the hall and had a more lived-in atmosphere.

'Come now, this is much better!' she remarked encouragingly. 'You stay here, Mama, with Theo and the girls, while Mrs Ibstone shows me the bedrooms, so that I can decide where we are all going to sleep.'

Mrs Ibstone paused in the act of lighting more candles to look at her, and then past her to Mrs Mallory. She said with unnecessary emphasis: 'I'd have thought the *mistress* would want to decide that.'

'My mother is very tired, and Master Theodore unwell after so many hours in the coach,' Dione said with finality, 'and I can assure you that both they and my sisters will be quite happy to leave this to me. That is so, is it not, Mama?' she added cheerfully.

'Oh yes, my love. Do whatever you think best,' Mrs Mallory replied faintly. 'Theo, my dearest, pull that little stool close beside me, and sit down so that you may rest your head in my lap. Take your cap off, dear, and then you can be comfortable.'

It was plain that her whole attention and concern was centred upon her son, and Mrs Ibstone, with an audible, contemptuous sniff, waddled out of the room again and led Dione back across the hall and, with much puffing and wheezing and pausing for breath, up the stairs to the bedrooms.

The first of these was quite large, with the same sort of ancient panelling and cavernous fireplace as the hall, and also the most forbidding bed Dione had ever seen. A four-poster which must have been made in Tudor times, with massive columns, tester and headboard all ornately carved, and curtains of dark, moth-eaten tapestry. It brooded like some squat monster in the middle of the room, flanked by lesser pieces of furniture of the same period—a tall cupboard, a couple of chests, a stool or two—and seemed to repel rather than invite repose.

'This is the Great Bedchamber,' Mrs Ibstone informed her. 'Master always slept here, so I reckon the mistress'll have it now.'

Dione tried to picture her nervous little mother sleeping in that catafalque of a bed, and knew that Mrs Mallory would never agree to such a thing. The prospect did not much appeal to Dione herself, but if anyone had to have this room, and apparently someone did, it would have to be she. She said nothing, however, but waited to see what the other rooms on the first floor were like.

They were not much of an improvement on the first, though not quite so oppressive. The best two were on the opposite side of the house, while another, and much much smaller one, adjoined the Great Bedchamber, with a connecting door between. Dione inspected them all and then announced her decision.

'I will take the Great Bedchamber, as you call it, and

my brother will have the small one adjoining it. The one at the corner of the house for my mother, and my sisters will share the large one next to it.'

'*You* be taking the Great Bedchamber, miss?' Mrs Ibstone's astonishment was genuine, but her tone suggested that Dione was committing a serious crime. 'Whatever will the mistress say?'

'Let me explain the situation to you, Mrs Ibstone,' Dione said quietly, 'so that there can be no misunderstanding. My mother does not enjoy good health, and finds day-to-day household cares too much for her, so in all such matters you will be dealing with me. As for the bedrooms, my little brother has, unhappily, inherited his mama's delicate constitution and is, moreover, only just recovering from a serious illness. He does not sleep well, and if he is restless in the night it is better that I should be disturbed than she. Besides, my mother is of a somewhat nervous disposition, and I do not think that she would care for the Great Bedchamber.'

'Nervous, is she?' the housekeeper remarked with a sniff. 'Reckon she's come to the wrong place, then.'

'Indeed?' Dione spoke sharply, but if the woman had hoped to hear alarm in her voice, she was disappointed; there was only displeasure. 'What, pray, do you mean by that?'

Mrs Ibstone shrugged. 'This be a very old house, miss, and there's some queer tales told of it.'

'Spectres with rattling chains, no doubt!' Dione retorted sceptically. 'Let me make one more thing plain to you, Mrs Ibstone. If I discover that you, or anyone else in this house, has been frightening my mother with such nonsense, I shall be very seriously displeased.'

Mrs Ibstone gave her a venomous look but made no reply, and Dione, who did not feel nearly as confident as she had contrived to appear, breathed an inward sigh of relief. She foresaw a continuing battle with the housekeeper, who so clearly resented their presence, but she felt that in their first encounter, the honours had gone to her.

* * *

Dione was to learn, during the course of that evening, just how wearing the struggle was going to be. There was a great deal to do; bedding to be fetched and aired, beds to be made up and bags unpacked; supper had to be prepared, since the family had eaten little during their journey, but Mrs Ibstone declared flatly that if she was expected to get a meal she could not attend to anything else, nor could her daughter, Molly, manage all the rest on her own.

If the housekeeper expected to floor her new mistress with this ultimatum, she did not succeed. Miss Mallory said promptly that she and her sisters were all perfectly capable of making up a bed or wielding a duster, and would Ibstone be good enough meanwhile to light a fire in the parlour for Mrs Mallory and Master Theo. Confronted by Molly Ibstone, a good-looking slattern in her early twenties, with luxuriant black curls, a high complexion, and ample curves which would probably, in time, equal her mother's girth, Dione took her measure at once. Molly was disposed to be insolent, looked with scorn at Miss Mallory's shabby attire, and was plainly contemptuous of the young ladies' readiness to help with the necessary arrangements, but she soon discovered that appearances were deceptive. During the years at her aunt's home, Dione had found herself more and more in the position of housekeeper, and had learned long ago how to deal with recalcitrant servants. Molly's pertness was rapidly reduced to sulky silence, and Dione could congratulate herself on another minor victory, though she doubted whether Molly's all too obvious indolence would be as easy to overcome.

Self-congratulation, however, was not her paramount emotion when, much later, she sat beside her brother's bed in the little room adjoining her own. It was nearly midnight, for Theodore, overtired and overwrought, had dozed and wakened and dozed again, restless in the strange bed. He missed the noise of the city where he had lived for nearly half his life, yet was disturbed by other, alien noises which broke the country quiet; the sighing of the wind, the hoot of an owl, a mysterious tapping at the window which proved, upon investigation, to be caused by a strand of wisteria trailing across it. Dione was worried, for it seemed to her that he was a little feverish, and she dreaded a recurrence of the illness which had given them so much anxiety a month or so ago.

As she sat there she was plagued again by doubts of the wisdom of her determination to come to Garth House. She was bone-weary, and a prey to that lowness of spirit engendered by fatigue and loneliness and the lateness of the hour, and it seemed to her at that moment that the only course open to her was to try to retrace the disastrous step she had taken. She could not expect Mama and the girls and Theodore to live in this tumbledown ruin of a house; she would have to abase herself; beg Aunt Winton to forgive her, and admit to Eustace that he knew best. She did not doubt that the breach could be healed. They would be able to return to the comfort and security of the Winton house, and though by doing so she would be committing herself to a marriage which she regarded with dismay and a faint revulsion, that was the price she must be prepared to pay to ensure the future well-being of those who depended upon her.

At last Theodore sank into a sounder sleep, and Dione decided that she could safely leave him. Wearily she undressed and climbed into the awe-inspiring bed, trying not to wonder whether Cousin Jonathan had died in it. It was unexpectedly comfortable, and she was just sliding into sleep when she was dragged back to consciousness by her brother's voice, muted yet urgent.

'Dee! Dee, are you asleep? I can hear something.'

With a sigh Dione sat up and groped for her dressing-gown. She had left the connecting door ajar and a candle burning, and when she entered the smaller room she found Theodore sitting up in bed, his blue eyes enormous in his thin face.

'What is it this time, Theo?' she asked, trying to keep the impatience from her voice. 'I heard nothing.'

'*I* did! A tapping sound, and—!'

'That was the creeper against the window.'

'No, it wasn't like that. This was indoors, and it was slower and—and *heavier*, and there were voices, too. It woke me up. Listen!'

They both listened. The wind soughed in the trees and the fingers of the wisteria patted the window-panes, but within the house there was silence. After a moment or two Dione said reassuringly:

'You were dreaming, love. Go back to sleep, there's a good boy.'

He slid down again on to the pillows that she had shaken up for him, saying, not in any rebellious spirit but simply as a statement of fact:

'I did hear it. It wasn't a dream, but I'm sorry that I disturbed you. Good night, Dee.'

'Good night, dear.' She tucked the covers more snugly around him and waited for a minute or two beside the bed, until she was sure that he had settled down again. She was almost reeling with fatigue as she went back to her own room and crept into bed again, but just before sleep claimed her she had a startlingly vivid recollection of Sir Greydon, of the striking, swarthy face and humorous manner, and of the blank disbelief in his eyes when she told him they were bound for Garth House.

'He knew,' was her last waking thought. 'He knew what it is like here. That is why he was so astonished . . .'

Part 2

Garth House, seen in full daylight, seemed at once less sinister and more dilapidated than it had appeared the previous night, when candlelight had softened the full impact of the decay now clearly visible on every side. The worn and threadbare carpets; the moth-eaten hangings; the lighter patches against the panelling which indicated that pictures and furniture had been removed; the dust and cobwebs which lay thickly everywhere. It was a sight to daunt the most inveterate optimist, and yet Dione found that for some reason her despairing mood had vanished with the darkness, and a return to London no longer seemed inevitable.

'I fear,' she said, after a second and more extensive tour of the house, 'that Cousin Jonathan must have fallen upon hard times towards the end of his life, for it looks to me as though he was obliged to sell all his more valuable possessions. Everything that is left is very old, and much of it must have been here as long as the house.'

'I believe you are right, Dee,' Mrs Mallory agreed with a sigh. 'I remember it as an old-fashioned house, but I am sure it was more comfortably furnished than this, and it was certainly not as sombre.'

'It would be much less sombre, Mama,' Edwina

observed practically, 'if it were not so dirty. Only look at the windows! One can scarcely see out of them.'

'Just so!' Dione looked approvingly at her youngest sister. 'It is wonderful what sweeping and polishing can do, for only think of that horrid little house we lived in before we went to Aunt Winton's. It was quite dreadful when we first took it, but we made it very tolerable.'

'But a house of this size, Dee!' Mrs Mallory said dubiously. 'How can we ever make it fit to live in? I am sure the Ibstones cannot be prevailed upon to do very much, and you know we cannot afford to hire more servants.'

'Leave the Ibstones to me,' Dione replied cheerfully. 'I have already set Molly to work upon your bedchamber, Mama, and though she was not very pleased, it will perhaps teach her not to hang at my heels the whole time. She followed me about the house as though she were my shadow, giving me a great deal of quite unnecessary information when I would much have preferred to find things out for myself. She is lazy, and would rather talk than work, but I am very well able to deal with her.'

'I hope you may be, Dee, for I am quite sure that I am not, nor with her mother.'

'I think Mrs Ibstone resents us,' Cecilia put in in her soft, gentle voice. 'Do you suppose, Dee, that she thought Cousin Jonathan had no living relatives, and that she and her husband might have Garth House bequeathed to them?'

'Very likely, though if that were so one would think they would have kept it in better order. Do not look so despondent, Mama! After all, we need not use the whole house. Just the hall, and this parlour, and perhaps one other room downstairs, and our bedrooms. Cecy and Edwina and I can do a good deal ourselves, and perhaps when Molly sees that we do not intend to leave everything to her she will feel less ill-used and be more willing to work.'

'You are such a comfort to me, Dee,' Mrs Mallory said tremulously, taking Dione's hand and pressing it. 'To all of us! I do not know what we should do without you.'

'Well, for one thing, Mama, without me you would still be living comfortably in Aunt Winton's house instead of this derelict ruin,' Dione replied lightly. She hesitated, turning her own hand to clasp her mother's frail fingers, and after a moment continued more seriously: 'Do you wish to return there? Answer me honestly, love, for if you feel you cannot endure to remain at Garth House I will write to my aunt, begging her pardon, and to Eustace, confessing that I have made a dreadful mistake and asking him to forgive me and come to our rescue. I do not think he will refuse.'

'Oh, Dee, no!' Edwina exclaimed in a shocked tone before Mrs Mallory could reply. 'It would be like going back in disgrace, for you know how Aunt Winton would scold, and besides, if you did that, Eustace would expect you to marry him after all. You know he would!'

'Don't be impertinent, my child,' Dione said calmly. 'Whether or not I marry Eustace is no concern of yours.'

'Yes, it is, for it would make him my brother-in-law,' Edwina retorted rebelliously, 'and then he really would have some right to tell us all what to do.'

'Hush, my love! It is most improper for you to speak so,' Mrs Mallory reproved her, 'though I must confess, Dee, that what Edwina says is true. He *would* expect it, and you would be under an obligation to agree. Have you considered that?'

'Yes, Mama, I have, and to what, after all, would I be agreeing? To a far better match than a dowerless female like myself has any right to expect, to a man I know to have the highest principles. To be sure, we have not always agreed very well in the past, but I dare say we could learn to deal tolerably well together. So, if you wish it, I will sit down and write those letters immediately, and I dare say that in a very short while we can all be back in London.'

Mrs Mallory hesitated, her gaze searching her daughter's face. Dione maintained a cheerful expression but found it difficult to sustain her mother's regard, and after a moment Mrs Mallory shook her head.

'No, Dee,' she said gently, 'you and Eustace could never learn to agree. I realize that now. I think I always did, but the match seemed so excellent from a material point of view, and your aunt was so eager for it that I allowed myself to be persuaded. I would not wish you—any of you—to marry solely for the sake of worldly advantage. There must be *some* degree of liking, of understanding, if there is to be any hope of an amicable marriage. If you did accept Eustace, my love, it would be only for the sake of the rest of us, and neither I, nor your sisters, nor Theo either, if he were old enough to understand such matters, would permit you to sacrifice your happiness on our behalf. You are too dear to us.'

Cecilia and Edwina murmured emphatic agreement. Dione looked from one to the other, her eyes very bright, and pressed her mother's thin fingers, but merely said in a rallying tone:

'That is settled, then! We stay here, and do the best we can with the means at our disposal. For one thing, at least, we may be thankful. Not only does Mrs Ibstone appear to be a good cook, but I observed from a window upstairs that the vegetable garden is in good order, and she keeps poultry, too.'

'And pigs!' Theodore, who had been doing some exploring of his own, came into the room in time to hear his sister's last remark. 'I saw them in the orchard. Mama, this is a capital place! Wasn't it a good notion of Dee's to come and live here?'

Mrs Mallory looked at him. He was grubby and untidy, his nankeens and jacket streaked with dust and cobwebs, his tasselled cap pushed far back on his fair curls and his shoes caked with mud; but the listlessness which had been a persistent and worrying aftermath of his illness had disappeared, and there was even a trace of colour in his cheeks. This, in his mother's opinion, was a complete vindication of the decision which had just been made.

'Yes, my love, an excellent notion,' she agreed with a smile, and looked again at her eldest daughter. 'Dee's notions generally are.'

* * *

For the rest of that day, and all of the next, the Mallory girls flung themselves with enthusiasm into the task of bringing order to the chaos of Garth House. They began with the bedrooms, Dione keeping Molly up to scratch by working with her, first in Mrs Mallory's room and then the Great Bedchamber and Theodore's, while Cecilia and Edwina tackled the apartment they shared. Mrs Mallory protested that they were leaving her nothing to do, but Dione said, with her ready chuckle:

'Don't you believe it, love. From what I can discover there is scarcely a piece of linen in the house which does not need patching or darning, and since you are by far the best needlewoman among us, I assure you that there will be plenty for you to do.'

In proof of this she made a foray to the linen closet, and carried to the parlour an armful of sheets and pillowcases and tablecloths, with which her mother, who not only excelled at sewing but also enjoyed it, settled down quite happily. By evening there was a pile of beautifully mended articles to be put away, though an even larger pile still awaited attention. By that time, too, all four bedchambers were clean and shining and smelling of beeswax, and three decidedly weary young ladies could congratulate themselves upon a task well done.

That night Dione slept deeply and dreamlessly, and woke to find a finger of sunlight probing between her drawn bed-curtains. Cheered by this promise of better weather, she got up and looked from the window, seeing the wilderness of garden quite transformed, a place of sunshine and dancing shadows, loud with birdsong. The pool, its surface rippled by the fresh breeze, sparkled and danced, and a wild duck with a miniature flotilla of ducklings about her swam slowly along the edge of the reedbed. Dione's spirits lifted yet further. She dressed quickly and tidied her room, and then quietly opened the door connecting it with Theodore's.

He was up and dressed, leaning at a perilous angle

from the window, which he had succeeded in forcing open, to peer along the wall beside it.

'I believe there is a bird's nest down there,' he informed his sister, drawing back into the room. 'Dee, I heard that sound again last night. The one that woke me the night before.'

Dione picked up his discarded nightshirt and folded it. 'What sound was that?'

'The tapping—not the creeper against the window, but the other. The heavier one, indoors. Did you not hear it?'

'No, and I very much doubt whether you did, either, except perhaps in a dream,' she retorted, beginning to make the bed. The window, left unattended, blew shut with a bang which made them both jump, and then swung wide again. 'But I did hear that! Close the window properly, Theo. We have enough broken panes already without chancing more.'

He turned to do as she said, but paused with his hand on the casement to look out again. 'There is a gap in the trees,' he remarked, 'and you can see right down the valley. There is a house there as big as a village.'

Dione laughed. 'Don't exaggerate, love!'

'But it is,' he insisted. 'Come and see.'

With a sigh of mock exasperation she joined him at the window, and looked in the direction he indicated. Framed by the bright foliage of early summer was a vista of sunlit valley, and in the middle distance, amid acres of parkland, a mansion of undoubtedly impressive proportions, surrounded by attendant outbuildings which did indeed lend it the appearance of a small village.

Dione chuckled again. 'Very well. I beg your pardon. Now do, pray close the window and make sure it is properly fastened before we go downstairs.'

He obeyed, but his curiosity had been aroused and later, when Molly brought breakfast into the parlour, he asked about the house they had seen. She replied sullenly, and with reluctance.

'That be the Abbey. Rushbourne Abbey.'

Theodore frowned. 'It doesn't look like an abbey.'

''Tis said it was, long since, so 'tis called that. 'Tis just a house now.'

'Who lives there?'

'Sir Greydon Varleigh—when he b'eant jaunting off to London or Brighton or some such place.'

Dione suppressed a start, and glanced quickly at Cecilia, seeing with exasperation but no surprise that colour had rushed up into her face so that she looked the picture of guilt. Fortunately, no one else was looking at her.

'Who is Sir Greydon Varleigh?' Theodore demanded.

Molly sniffed. 'Oh, he owns nigh on all the land in these parts—aye, and most of the folks, too, or so he thinks. Then there's his grandma, the old Dowager. She be as bad as him, or worse.'

'Theo, that is quite enough.' Dione roused herself to speak firmly. 'Thank you, Molly. You may go.'

Molly went, with something suspiciously like a flounce. As the door closed behind her, Theodore said reproachfully:

'Why did you stop her, Dee? It was interesting.'

'Yes, my love, but it is not at all the thing to be gossiping with the servants,' his mother put in mildly. 'Molly is already somewhat more encroaching than I could wish, and it will not do to encourage her.'

Theodore sighed, and applied himself to his breakfast, while Dione allowed her thoughts to wander. So their benefactor at the 'Royal George' was the great man of the district. Remembering his pleasant but unmistakable air of authority, and the way in which the landlord had obeyed him without question, she could not feel surprise, and yet there had been not the least height in his manner, nothing to justify the way in which Molly had spoken of him. 'The old Dowager' might well be a tartar, but it was hard to imagine the man who had shown kindness to two strange and totally insignificant young women behaving in a way which would cause a person of Molly Ibstone's station in life to take him in dislike.

That day the three girls, with Molly's unwilling

assistance, set to work on the parlour, and Mrs Mallory was obliged to carry her sewing up to her bedroom. The task occupied them for the whole of the day, but by early evening, when the furniture was all back in place and Cecilia had set a bowl of flowers on the table, the room had begun to look quite homelike.

'Excellent!' Dione said with satisfaction, surveying the transformation. 'Tomorrow we will tackle the hall. I will tell Ibstone to clear all those dead ashes from the fireplace—which I am sure has not been touched for many years—and then we will see what we can do to set the rest of it to rights.' She heard Cecilia give a small, weary sigh, and added sympathetically: 'Yes I know, love, but it is not the smallest use making the parlour and our bedrooms habitable if we have to walk through dirt and disorder every time we come into the house. We *must* set the hall to rights, but that will do for the present. Now let us make ourselves clean and tidy, for we cannot sit down to dinner in this state.'

They went upstairs together, and parted to go to their separate rooms, but a little later, when Dione, having washed and put on a clean gown, had just finished dressing her thick, gold-brown hair, her mother came into her room from the small adjoining chamber. She looked worried.

'Dee, where is Theo?'

'Downstairs, I expect, Mama, waiting for his dinner. It is wonderful how his appetite has improved these two days past.'

'He is not in the parlour,' Miss Mallory said uneasily, 'and Molly assures me he has been nowhere near the kitchen or the yard. I thought you must have sent him upstairs to make himself clean and tidy.'

'And *I* thought you had probably done so, though, had I stopped to think, I would have realized that it is a deal too quiet in his room for him to be there. He must still be in the garden, then. Did you call to him?'

'No, for I felt sure he was in the house. I have been sewing in my room, and have not seen him all the afternoon.'

It occurred to Dione that she had not seen Theodore either, though this did not seem to be any cause for disquiet. It was a beautiful day, and the big, overgrown gardens, utterly unlike anything he had ever known, seemed to fascinate him. He had gone out immediately after breakfast, reappeared briefly at midday in search of sustenance, and then hurried out of doors again.

'I will go and look for him,' she said soothingly. 'Do not fret, Mama! We must be thankful to see him so active and occupied.'

'Oh, I am, Dee, believe me, but it will not do for him to be overtiring himself. You know the doctor warned us most particularly against that. When did you last see him?'

'When we ate our luncheon,' Dione admitted. 'After that we were busy in the parlour.'

'Dee!' Mrs Mallory exclaimed in dismay. 'That was hours ago!'

'Yes, love, but you know what Theo is like when he becomes absorbed in anything. Time means nothing to him at all. I will go and find him.'

She took a shawl from one of the chests and cast it about her shoulders, then slipped an arm through her mother's and drew her towards the door, added cheerfully:

'You go and wait in the parlour, Mama. What, by the by, do you think of our efforts there?'

'Oh, a wonderful difference, my dear! It looks almost as I remember it,' Mrs Mallory replied, but her tone was abstracted, and Dione halted again and turned to face her.

'What is it, Mama? Come now, confess! You cannot be so worried just because Theo has stayed too long out of doors.'

'I keep thinking of the pool,' Mrs Mallory admitted reluctantly. 'We were all busy in the house, and if he had fallen in—!'

'Mama dear, Theo is not a baby. He is a sensible little boy, and in any event, I warned him not to go near the pool. No, he has probably found some hideaway among the trees and is busy fancying himself to be Robin Hood or some such thing, for you know how he loves such play-acting. However, he ought to have come indoors by now, and you may be sure I shall rake him down severely for not doing so.'

Somewhat reassured, Mrs Mallory accompanied her downstairs and returned to the parlour, while Dione went on across the hall and out through the front door. On the steps she paused, looking about her, surprised and a little dismayed to see that the sun had already dipped behind the trees, so that the house and gardens lay in shadow. She had not realized it was so late.

She called her brother's name several times, then, when there was no reply, went across the weed-grown gravel and along the least overgrown of the paths leading from it. Methodically she worked her way round the gardens, calling repeatedly but winning no response. Then, despising herself yet aware of growing uneasiness, walked slowly around the whole perimeter of the pool, noting with relief that the reeds still stood straight and undisturbed and that there were no footprints in the muddy verges of the water.

She tried to remember what Theodore had talked about at luncheon. The fountain in the rose-garden was broken, and he did not suppose (hopefully) that it could be made to work again; he had seen a thrush's nest; he had found the place where the stream ran into the pool and had to be crossed by stepping-stones; there was a path beside it, leading up into the woods. Where, did they suppose, did the stream come from?

Dione stopped short as that last memory returned to her. She had just passed that spot herself, picking her way somewhat apprehensively across the moss-grown stones set amid hurrying water, and now she felt convinced that Theodore had yielded to the temptation to go in search of the stream's source, pretending as he did so that he was an intrepid explorer braving the dangers of an unknown land.

She went back to the house by way of the stableyard and the domestic quarters. In the kitchen Mrs Ibstone was preparing dinner, and glared at her with undisguised hostility, but Dione was unmoved by this reception and inquired the whereabouts of Ibstone himself, for she had formed the intention of sending him to look for Theodore in the woods behind the house. Mrs Ibstone, with evident satisfaction, informed her that her husband had gone to town and had not yet returned.

'It being market-day, and things needed,' she added accusingly, her tone implying that, but for the intrusion of the Mallory family, Ibstone would not have been put to so much trouble. 'He had to take the cart, so like as not he won't be home till after dark. That old horse can't be hurried.'

Dione thought it more likely that Ibstone was amusing himself with his cronies at some inn or tavern, but she was by now too concerned about Theodore to pursue the matter. Telling the housekeeper that dinner would probably have to be delayed, she went through to the front of the house and put her head round the door of the parlour, where Mrs Mallory had now been joined by Cecilia and Edwina.

'I have not found Theo yet, but I believe I know where he has wandered off to,' Dione told them lightly, 'so I will just go and fetch him. I have desired Mrs Ibstone to hold dinner for us.'

She withdrew quickly before her mother could ask any awkward questions.

* * *

The path beside the stream was narrow and muddy, but at first it was easy enough. After a couple of hundred yards, however, it began to climb, gently at first and then more steeply, snaking upward over rocks and protruding tree-roots. Branches hung low and undergrowth encroached upon it—later in the summer it would be impassable—and before long Dione was hot and breathless and as much angry as concerned. Twice she halted and called her brother's name, but her voice echoed desolately through the wood without evoking any response.

Eventually, reaching a point where the massive, ivy-festooned trunk of a fallen tree overhung the path at a perilous angle, completely blocking it, she paused in dismay, for it seemed that she had guessed wrongly. Theodore could not have come this way after all. If he had, she would have met him returning, for she had seen no other path. Perhaps he had gone instead along the drive, and the road towards the village; perhaps he was even now safely at home, waiting impatiently for his dinner while his eldest sister slipped and stumbled through these precipitous woodlands on a fool's errand. At that moment she felt that she could readily have boxed his ears, and she was just turning to retrace her steps when a gleam of bright metal at the edge of the path caught her eye. Stooping, she picked up a button instantly recognizable as belonging to Theodore's jacket.

For a moment she stared at it in the fading light, and then called his name again as loudly as she could, but to no avail. Yet he had undoubtedly been here, and since she had not met him coming back, he must somehow have gone on. She took a closer look at the fallen tree, and decided that there was just one place, immediately above the spot where she had found the button, where the obstacle might be surmounted. In the ordinary way she would never have considered attempting such a feat, but she could not rid herself of the fear that Theodore might be lying injured somewhere ahead, so, since there was no fear of anyone witnessing her immodesty, she knotted the shawl firmly about her shoulders, kilted her skirts above the knee, and, grasping a protruding branch, managed to haul herself up on to the tree-trunk.

Her most immediate fear, of finding her brother lying senseless on the far side, was not realized. The path was deserted, winding upwards and out of sight around a bluff of rock, and though for some while she had been unable to see the stream, and only to hear it faintly, the sound of falling water was now close at hand. Glancing back the way she had come, she made an unwelcome discovery. To climb up to her present perch had been difficult; to climb down the same way, from a tree-trunk overhanging a steep drop, would be impossible. Come what might, she would have to go on.

She slid cautiously and inelegantly down the far side of the tree, uttering an exclamation of dismay as her skirt caught, and then pulled free with a rending sound. Reaching the ground, she ruefully inspected the damage, then, holding up the torn and trailing flounces, set off wearily along the path. Every step was an effort now, but it was perhaps fortunate that she was not hurrying, for the path dipped abruptly as it rounded the bluff and she found herself unexpectedly on the brink of a broad, shallow pool, fed by a spring which appeared to rise somewhere in the rocky bank above. This, then, was the source which Theodore must have been seeking.

The path skirted the pool and then sloped away from it, much less steeply and more clearly defined, across the hillside rather than up it. Dione picked her way carefully past the water and trudged on, emerging a few minutes later into a lane, beyond which lay rolling grassland. To her right the road ran straight for several hundred yards, to her left it began to descend, soon passing out of sight behind the trees; it was deserted, and there was no habitation of any kind to be seen. The sun had set, and though it was less dark here than in the woods, Dione was uneasily aware of the deepening shadows, and of the fact that she had not the faintest idea how far she was from Garth House. Sinking wearily down on the grassy bank beside the road she faced the unpalatable fact that not only had she failed to find Theodore, even though he must certainly have passed this way, she had also come uncomfortably close to losing herself, stranded as she now was on a deserted hilltop in gathering darkness.

Since there could be no question of returning through the woods, she would have to follow the road, and hope that she would come soon to some farm or cottage where she could seek assistance; and a fine impression she would make, she reflected grimly, bareheaded and dishevelled, with her gown torn and stained with mud and moss. She sighed and got up, wrapping her shawl more closely about her, for here on the hill top in the deepening dusk the air seemed suddenly cold, and began to walk down the hill, but had barely gone fifty yards when she heard the sound of a carriage coming behind her. She looked quickly round, but when she saw that it was a curricle and four bearing two masculine figures her heart lurched unpleasantly, and her anxiety about Theodore was suddenly superseded by disquiet on her own account. In a moment of panic she wondered if it would be prudent to beat a hurried retreat into the woods, but the path was out of reach and the slope behind her too steep to make flight practicable; then the curricle was close enough for her to distinguish the features of its occupants, and with an illogical surge of relief she recognized the driver as Sir Greydon Varleigh.

The horses were moving at a brisk trot, and for one alarming moment she thought he was going to drive straight past her, but even as she lifted a hand he recognized her and reined in his team. One swift, comprehensive glance took in her dishevelled state, and he said quickly:

'You need assistance, ma'am. What has happened?'

She explained as briefly as she could, vexed to find that her voice was shaking. Sir Greydon cast an astonished glance past her into the thickening darkness of the woods.

'You have climbed up from Garth House? My dear ma'am, you must be exhausted! Permit me to drive you back there at once.'

He added a word to his groom, who immediately jumped down from the curricle to make room for Dione and to assist her up into it. She hesitated, looking up anxiously at Sir Greydon.

'You are exceedingly kind, sir, but my brother—!'

'Is almost certainly ahead of us on the road,' he replied reassuringly, 'in which case we can take him up also. We may even find that he has already reached Garth House.'

She recognized the truth of these words, and allowed herself to be helped up into the curricle. The groom climbed up behind, and Sir Greydon put his horses in motion again, observing as he did so:

'Once your brother reached this lane, ma'am, he

should have had little difficulty in finding his way back to Garth House. How old is he?'

'Eleven.' She saw his brows lift, and added defensively: 'You think I am refining too much upon a prank by a boy of that age, but Theo has never been strong, and has only lately recovered from a serious illness. I cannot help fearing that he may have had a fall, or even have been overcome by exhaustion, and not heard me calling to him.'

'You do not think he may have heard you, and remained silent out of sheer devilment, just to tease you? Boys do play such tricks, you know.'

'Not Theo,' Dione replied with conviction. 'Oh, he might have done so in the garden, but not after I had followed him all the way through the woods. And he had certainly climbed that path, or I would not have found the button from his jacket.'

'Very true. If we do not find him at Garth House, or on the way there, a search must be made for him immediately. My name, by the by, is Varleigh. Sir Greydon Varleigh, of Rushbourne Abbey, just beyond Brambledon. I take it that you, ma'am, now reside at Garth House?'

'Yes, I am Dione Mallory. My father was Mr Jonathan Mallory's cousin, which is how Theo came to inherit the house.' She paused, but after a moment added in a low voice. 'It was my notion to come here. If any harm has befallen him, I shall never forgive myself.'

She had forgotten that she was addressing a stranger—was scarcely aware, in fact, that she had spoken her thought aloud—and was therefore almost startled when Greydon Varleigh answered her. Both tone and words were a matter of fact, but she was aware of a welcome note of sympathy in his voice.

'There is very little reason, ma'am, to suppose that any harm *has* befallen him, but if he really is missing, it will be the simplest thing in the world to have a search made for him. I will see to it immediately should it prove necessary.'

'*You* will?' Dione was taken aback. 'You are exceedingly kind, sir, but I could not permit you to be put to so much trouble on our account. We are not even acquainted.'

'We are neighbours, are we not?' he countered in an amused tone. 'I was under the impression that we are becoming better acquainted every minute, and besides, you would find it very difficult to organize such a search yourself since you are a stranger in Brambledon. I cannot feel that Jack Ibstone would be much assistance.'

'I am sure of it, even if he were at home, which he is not,' Dione agreed roundly, 'but even so, I—that is, Mama would not wish to place herself under such an obligation.'

'Miss Mallory,' Sir Greydon informed her calmly, 'you are talking nonsense, which I can only ascribe to the fatigue and anxiety which you must undoubtedly be feeling. We must hope that the necessity of arranging for a search-party will not arise, but if it does, you will leave the entire matter to me.'

There was a pause, during which a sidelong glance at the lady informed him that she was labouring under strong emotion, torn between indignation and a sense of obligation for the assistance he was already rendering her. His lips twitched, for he possessed a lively sense of the ridiculous, and though he could sympathize with her anxiety he could not really believe it to be justified. Before she could think of anything to say, however, they rounded a bend to see two youthful male figures a hundred yards or so ahead of them, walking in the same direction.

'Ah!' Sir Greydon said with satisfaction. 'Miss Mallory, is either of those young gentlemen the brother you have mislaid?'

'Yes, it is.' There was overwhelming relief in Dione's voice, but a touch of perplexity also, for though the smaller boy was undoubtedly Theodore, there seemed, even in the gathering darkness, to be something a little odd in his appearance. 'What in the world has he been up to?'

The boys looked round as the curricle approached and

then moved to the side of the road, and as Sir Greydon brought the carriage to a halt beside them, Theodore's curious appearance was explained. He was soaking wet, his clothes sodden and dripping, his cap gone and his fair curls plastered to his head.

'Theo!' Dione exclaimed in distress. 'Good heavens, what have you been doing?'

'Dee!' Theodore was staring at her in the blankest astonishment. 'What are *you* doing in that bang-up curricle?'

'Looking for you, you abominable boy! I have been searching for you all through the woods, and it is only thanks to this gentleman's kindness in offering me a seat in his carriage that I am not trudging along the road after you as well.' She glanced at Sir Greydon. 'This is my brother, Theodore, sir. Theo, make your bow to Sir Greydon Varleigh.'

Theodore obeyed. Sir Greydon, who was having some difficulty in keeping his countenance, solemnly acknowledged the introduction, but added briskly:

'I fancy, my lad, that the sooner you are at home and out of those wet clothes, the better it will be. Stubbs, help him up.' He removed the light rug which covered his legs, and which the groom had carefully arranged around Dione also. 'I think we must sacrifice this, ma'am. Your brother's need is clearly greater than ours.'

She agreed gratefully, for though Theodore appeared to be in good spirits he had spoken through chattering teeth, and when the groom helped him up to the seat beside her, she could tell how violently he was shivering. While she wrapped the rug closely about him Sir Greydon surveyed the other boy, a sturdy, ruddy-complexioned lad as fair as Theodore himself.

'You are young Durridge, are you not?'

'That I be, your Honour. Jem Durridge.' The boy knuckled his forehead as he spoke, then nodded towards Theodore. 'I were just taking him home. He asked me the way to Garth House, but I thought as I'd better see him safe to the door, him being a stranger, and nobbut a young'un.' He was no more than thirteen himself.

'Very proper,' Sir Greydon agreed gravely, and Dione smiled warmly at Master Durridge and thanked him for his help. Then, as the curricle moved off again, she asked in a resigned tone:

'What happened, Theo? I suppose you fell into the pool?'

He nodded, rather shamefacedly. 'Yes. I was climbing up the bank to see where the water came from, and I slipped. Then I tried to go back home through the woods, but I couldn't get down over the fallen tree.' A thought appeared to strike him. 'Dee, you did not climb up over that, did you? I don't see how you could, in those long skirts.'

'Well, I certainly did not *fly* over it!' Dione spoke with some asperity, for her close proximity to Sir Greydon, occasioned by Theodore's additional presence in the carriage, informed her that his shoulders were shaking with suppressed laughter. He must have a very clear idea of how she had managed the climb, she thought, and felt her cheeks grow hot with embarrassment. What a hoyden she must seem to him, scrambling about in woods, and accepting without hesitation a seat in the carriage of a stranger.

The journey back to Garth House was soon accomplished. The lane descended the hill in a series of sweeping bends, and at the foot of it joined the road along which the Mallory family had approached their inheritance two days before. Sir Greydon maintained a brisk pace until the gates of the house were reached, but was then obliged to restrain his horses to a walk, for it was almost completely dark beneath the trees, while the rutted drive and overhanging branches were additional hazards.

The house, when they reached it, looked almost as inhospitable as when Dione had first seen it, except that the front door stood open and a light was burning dimly in the hall. As hooves and wheels crunched on the gravel there was movement there also, and Edwina appeared in the doorway, peering rather nervously into the gloom. Dione spoke quickly to reassure her.

'We are home, Edwina. Fetch Mama, if you please.'

The curricle came to a halt and Stubbs jumped down and went to the horses' heads, while Sir Greydon lifted Theodore down and assisted Dione to alight. As she led the way into the hall, Mrs Mallory, with Edwina and Cecilia at her heels, came hurrying from the direction of the parlour, to utter a cry of dismay as she saw the state her son was in.

'Mama!' Dione broke in firmly upon the flurry of anxious exclamations and questions. 'This gentleman is Sir Greydon Varleigh, who has been kind enough to come to our rescue and drive us home. My mother, sir, and my sisters, Cecilia and Edwina.'

The girls curtsied. Mrs Mallory acknowledged the introduction in a flustered way and thanked Sir Greydon profusely, but her thoughts were clearly centred upon her son. Sir Greydon felt that he could not blame her; seen in the light, Theodore's face was white and pinched with cold, with an ominous, bluish tinge about the lips, and he was shivering uncontrollably.

'I am happy to have been of service, ma'am, but pray do not let me intrude upon you now. Theodore needs dry clothes and a warm bed if he is not to take a chill, so I will not delay in bidding you goodnight.'

She agreed with relief, thanked him again and hurried her son away up the stairs. Sir Greydon turned to Dione, adding with a smile:

'And I trust that you, Miss Mallory, will suffer no ill effects from this evening's misadventure.'

'Oh, I do not suppose it, sir! I am very rarely ill.' She held out her hand, looking up at him with that frank directness which had appealed to him at their first meeting. 'Thank you for everything. I am very sensible of the debt I owe you.'

He shook his head, but grasped her fingers lightly for a moment before bowing and turning towards the door. Dione hesitated, then took a pace after him, saying in a low voice.

'One more favour, Sir Greydon. Can you tell me if there is a reliable physician in this neighbourhood?' She cast a worried glance over her shoulder towards the stairs. 'I fear we may have need of one.'

'Dr Bamfield lives in the village, ma'am. He has attended our family for many years, and I have heard my grandmother recommend him in the strongest terms. Do you wish me to send a message requesting him to call upon you?'

She assented gratefully, and watched him go down the steps and mount into the curricle. The light carriage swept round in a smooth semicircle and disappeared into the dark mouth of the drive. Dione closed the door and turned to confront the critical gaze of her youngest sister, Cecilia having followed their mother and brother up the stairs.

'You look the most complete romp, Dee,' Edwina informed her candidly. 'There is dirt on your face, your hair is coming down and your gown is badly torn. It is as well Mama was too fussed about Theo to notice, but what such a tremendous swell as Sir Greydon must have thought I cannot imagine.'

Dione usually took sisterly criticism in her stride, but on this occasion she gave way to a most unaccustomed spurt of temper. 'Be quiet, Edwina, and do not use such vulgar expressions,' she said irritably. 'I am tired and I am hungry and in no mood to listen to impertinence from you. Go and see if you can make yourself useful to Mama.'

Edwina blinked, and went. It was debatable whether she or Dione was the more surprised.

* * *

Rushbourne Abbey, where Sir Greydon arrived just after dark, had been the home of the Varleigh family ever since the first Sir Greydon married the heiress of Rushbourne in the closing years of the sixteenth century. He had been something of an adventurer, that Elizabethan Varleigh, one of those English sea-dogs who continually challenged the might of Spain in order to plunder the rich lands of the New World, and he had plundered to some purpose, founding a fortune which he presently augmented by that advantageous marriage. Thus he had risen from being merely the younger son of an obscure country squire to a position of wealth and power, master of one of those broad estates wrested from the Church by King Henry VIII and bestowed upon certain of his loyal and trusted followers.

Of the original abbey nothing now remained above ground, and only its name and a labyrinth of stone-vaulted cellars recalled its monastic origin. The Tudor mansion which had replaced it had been embellished and added to by successive generations, and was now a sprawling pile composed of many different styles of architecture which somehow blended into a picturesque and not unpleasing whole. The main entrance was in the imposing west front, and it was here that Sir Greydon alighted, telling his head groom to drive the curricle round to the stables.

Stubbs obeyed in a thoughtful and perplexed frame of mind, a state which had been growing upon him ever since leaving London a week before. Most members of the huge staff of servants needed to keep Rushbourne functioning smoothly were not very well acquainted with the adult Greydon Varleigh, for he had entered the army at the age of eighteen, and served under Wellington throughout the Peninsular Wars and the Waterloo campaign, only selling out after the final defeat of Napoleon, but Stubbs had been with him since his boyhood and throughout his military career. He was completely devoted to Sir Greydon's interests and could be depended upon to obey any command, no matter how eccentric, and keep his inevitable reflections to himself, but he was sorely puzzled by his master's present behaviour.

During the three years since leaving the army, Sir Greydon had become one of the acknowledged leaders of fashion, yet here he was, at the height of the London Season, isolating himself at his country seat for no reason that Stubbs could discover. They had left London at a moment's notice, immediately following a visit from Mr Mayhew, Sir Greydon's agent at Rushbourne, and

Stubbs had naturally supposed that something was very much amiss at the Abbey, and yet all appeared to be well. Stubbs was at a loss, just as he was at a loss to understand why the past week had been spent riding or driving from place to place in the surrounding countryside and never halting for long at any of them, but he knew beyond doubt that Sir Greydon was worried, and that his disquiet was increasing as time passed. It was true that this evening's encounter with the rather odd Miss Mallory and her tiresome young brother had briefly diverted him, but almost immediately after leaving Garth House he had relapsed into his former preoccupation.

Sir Greydon, meanwhile, unaware of his henchman's anxious speculation, had gone up the wide, shallow steps to the door, both leaves of which were thrown open at his approach by a pair of footmen. The dignified form of his butler advanced to greet him, and announced, as he relieved Sir Greydon of hat, gloves and driving coat:

'Mr Calderwood arrived during your absence, sir. He is in the library.'

He saw Sir Greydon's black brows come together in a frown, as though the arrival of his cousin was unwelcome as well as unexpected, but he merely said:

'Thank you, Dobson. I will have a word with him before I go upstairs.'

In the library a dark haired, fashionably attired young man was lounging with long legs outstretched and a glass in his hand, but he set this down and rose to his feet as Sir Greydon came in. He was nearly as tall as his host, but of more slender build and four or five years younger, with sufficient resemblance to Sir Greydon to mark him as a member of the same family. He threw up one hand like a fencer acknowledging a hit, and said with a grin:

'Don't eat me, Grey! I'm here under protest, and if I am intruding upon you will go away at once, with no more said.'

'That I find difficult to believe,' Varleigh replied ironically, waving his visitor back to his seat. 'Upon what do you imagine you *are* intruding?'

'My dear fellow, how can *I* tell? What's more, as I told

Mama, it's no concern of mine if you choose to cancel all your engagements in the middle of the Season, and take yourself off to Rushbourne without a word to anyone.'

'I take it that my aunt did not agree with you?'

'Well, you know what females are for curiosity, and besides, she was depending upon you to attend the ball she was giving for my sister. Charlotte, too! She'd set her heart on dancing with Cousin Greydon at her come-out. Been puffing it off to her friends for weeks.'

Sir Greydon struck himself lightly on the forehead. 'Confound it all! I did promise her that, didn't I? Poor little Charlotte! I'll have to find some way to make it up to her.'

'Oh, that will be easy enough,' Mr Calderwood replied airily. 'Squire her to Almack's one night instead, and she'll soon forgive you.'

'I trust that she will, but this does not explain, my dear Vivyan, what brings you here. Surely you did not drive all the way from London merely to take me to task for Charlotte's disappointment?'

'No, nor to pry into your concerns, coz, I give you my word. At least'—he corrected himself hastily—'I would not have done if our respected grandmama had not busied herself in the affair. She's devilish displeased with you, Grey! I can't recall seeing her more put about.'

Greydon frowned. 'I wrote to her the day after I arrived here.'

'Yes—telling her that a matter of business had obliged you to go into the country for a time. You can't have been fool enough to suppose that would satisfy the old lady?' He did not wait for a reply, but added rather uncomfortably—for Greydon was looking decidedly grim: 'In the end, nothing would do but for me to agree to come and find out what is going on. I didn't want to, and told her you wouldn't like it, but she wouldn't take no for an answer. She was working herself into such a fury I thought I'd better agree, for Mama had told me it doesn't do now for her to get into a fret.'

'No, it does not. Her doctor warned me, after that attack she had last summer, that another would almost certainly prove fatal, and that we must do all in our power to see that she is not upset in any way. You were right to do as she wished, though I cannot for the life of me understand why she should be so put about simply because I absent myself from town for a week or two.'

'Cannot understand?' Vivyan stared at him. 'Dash it all, Grey, you know this obsession she has about the name not dying out. "The last of the Varleighs" and all that flummery.'

'I know, but I do not see—!' Greydon broke off, staring in his turn. 'Good God! She has not taken it into her head that I am involved in an affair of honour?'

'Don't think that had occurred to her,' Vivyan said hastily. 'At least, it hadn't when I took leave of her.' He eyed his cousin warily. 'You're not, are you?'

'Of course I am not,' Greydon replied impatiently, 'but if our grandmother is not imagining me slain in a duel, why is she so disturbed by my absence?'

'Confound it all, Grey! At such a time—Grandmama seemed to think it was as good as settled.' He saw that Sir Greydon was genuinely perplexed, and drew a deep breath. 'Grey, you can tell me to go to the devil if you wish, but are you, or are you not, on the point of offering for Priscilla Marstow?'

Sir Greydon continued to regard him, but now the bewilderment in his eyes had been replaced by a kind of exasperated understanding.

'Is that what Grandmama told you?'

Vivyan nodded. 'Said you had given her your word. Of course, I didn't believe *that*, for I know what Grandmama is like in one of her high flights, and I cannot imagine that you would be influenced by anyone, or by anything but your own inclination, in such a matter, but something must have put the notion into her head.'

'Oh, yes!' There was a tinge of bitterness in Greydon's voice. 'You see, Vivyan, our grandmother is seventy-eight years old and in precarious health, and, as you know, she has this obsession about the Varleigh name. Ever since I sold out she has been plaguing me to marry and provide Rushbourne with an heir, and when she was ill last year, and in great distress, I promised her that I would find a wife within a year.'

Vivyan regarded him curiously. 'And will you?'

'Naturally, since I have given my word, though not necessarily Miss Marstow. I wonder why Grandmama has fixed upon her?'

Vivyan grinned. 'Because only the best will do for a Varleigh, and Miss Marstow is the Season's most admired debutante. She has birth, beauty, a respectable fortune—!'

'And very little else.'

'Deuce take it, Grey! What more do you want?'

'Oh, I don't know!' Greydon went to the table where decanters stood on a silver tray, and poured a glass of wine. 'Vivyan, has it never occurred to you that all the girls from among whom we are expected to choose our brides are as insipidly alike as though they had been cast from the same mould? So full of feminine accomplishments that they have not one original thought in their heads, and must either coquet or languish. I have yet to meet one who is not hedged about by notions of propriety instilled by her mama and her governess until she is afraid to think or act for herself. At least—!' He paused, a sudden recollection bringing a reminiscent smile to his lips.

'At least—?' Vivyan was watching him, and spoke in a rallying tone. 'Come, Grey, out with it! At least—what?'

'Oh, nothing of any significance. I was merely recalling a young lady whom I recently encountered. The first time was the other evening at the "Royal George" where, having alighted from the London stage at the "Griffin", she had the temerity to approach Hobkin and seek to hire a carriage in which to complete her journey. Yes, and to take him severely to task when he refused to provide one!'

'Travelling alone by the stage?' Vivyan was disappointed. 'I thought you said "a young lady".'

'Unquestionably a lady. When we met, she was very properly chaperoned by a younger sister, and they were travelling, I gathered, with their mama and two younger members of the family, who were awaiting their return to the "Griffin" with the carriage.'

'Which I'll wager they did not obtain from Hobkin.'

'There was a little difficulty,' Greydon admitted. 'I was obliged to intervene, though I am not altogether convinced that the lady would not have prevailed, unaided, in the end.'

'Sounds an odd sort of female to me,' Vivyan remarked. 'Was she pretty?'

'Pretty?' Greydon paused, considering an unexpectedly vivid memory of Miss Mallory. 'No, not particularly. The younger sister would probably have appealed to you—one of those delicate, die-away blondes. But the truly odd circumstance was that they were bound for Brambledon. For Garth House.'

'What, old Mallory's place? Dash it all, Grey, it's a confounded ruin. What the devil could they want there?'

'I have since learned that they are the new owners. I recall that Mayhew told me there had been some difficulty in tracing Mallory's heir, which is why the house has yeen standing empty ever since the old man died. Empty, that is, except for the Ibstone family.'

'Heaven help the new owners, then!' Vivyan remarked flippantly. 'Wait a bit, though! You said you met this girl at the "Royal George" for the *first* time. Don't tell me you have seen her since?'

'Yes, though I would scarcely describe her as a girl, for she is, I should imagine, in her early twenties. I encountered her less than an hour ago on top of Garth Hill.'

Vivyan eyed him suspiciously. 'At this time in the evening? Grey, you're bamming me!'

'It's the truth, I give you my word. She had mislaid her young brother, and climbed up through the woods searching for him.' Greydon laughed at the expression in his cousin's face, and went on to describe his second encounter with Miss Mallory.

Vivyan was amused, but gave it as his opinion that such unconventional conduct would do her no good in some quarters. 'Can't see her being received by some of the old tabbies around here,' he said brutally. 'That crony of Mama's, Mrs Elverbury, for instance.' He paused, regarding his cousin with some indignation. 'Grey, why are we discussing Miss Mallory?'

Sir Greydon's lips twitched. 'I changed the subject,' he explained kindly. 'It seemed to me we were getting into somewhat deep waters.'

'Ah!' said Mr Calderwood intelligently. 'Telling me to mind my own business. I don't blame you, but tell me also what tale I am to carry to Grandmama. My orders were to command you back to town immediately.'

'Impossible!' Sir Greydon said decisively. 'Present my compliments to Grandmama, and assure her that I will inform her as soon as I find myself able to leave Rushbourne.'

'That won't do! Ten to one you will have her posting down here herself.'

'God forbid!' Greydon exclaimed fervently. 'I am devoted to Grandmama, but she must not be permitted to come to Rushbourne at present. Besides, why the devil should she? Even if I intended to offer for Miss Marstow, it is surely not a matter of urgency?'

'Ah, but it is, according to Grandmama! There are half a dozen men trying to fix their interest with the girl, and though she may have been waiting for *you* to cast the handkerchief in her direction, if she feels you have slighted her by going off in this fashion, it's quite likely that she will accept someone else. Riversdale's after her, and it's no secret that the Marstows favour him.'

'Have a fancy to see their daughter a Countess, have they?'

'The title's one consideration, of course,' Vivyan admitted with a grin, 'but I'm told they regard him as a more *stable* character than Sir Greydon Varleigh. You my dear fellow, may be a top-of-the-trees Corinthian, a buck of the first head, a nonpareil—!'

'Cut line, Viv, for God's sake!' Greydon protested, between amusement and annoyance. 'When have I ever claimed to be any of these?'

'Oh, you don't have to, Grey! It's a well-known fact,

and though it may appeal to Miss Priscilla, it don't appeal to her parents. Devilish straitlaced, the Marstows, and Riversdale's a deuced dull dog, as you know. So, according to Grandmama, if you don't bestir yourself you may find Miss Marstow betrothed to him by the time you do return to town.'

Greydon shrugged. 'Priscilla Marstow is not the only eligible female in London.'

'That's damned cold-blooded!' Vivyan protested. 'Don't you care one way or the other, even though you have been paying court to the girl?'

'My dear Vivyan, you are surely not suggesting that a romantic attachment is necessary, or even desirable, when it comes to marriage? Miss Marstow is very pretty and amiable, and no doubt would make a suitable wife, but the same can be said—though in varying degrees, I admit—of at least half the marriageable girls in town.'

Mr Calderwood was silent, dubiously regarding his cousin. He would have supposed Greydon to be jesting, had his voice not held a harshness that Vivyan had never heard in it before. It could be, of course, that he was regretting the promise he had made and irked by the prospect of giving up his bachelor existence, yet he must always have known that it was his duty to marry one day, for his parents and elder brother had died together, tragically, while he was still in the nursery, and there was no other direct male heir. Moreover, in the world in which he moved it was not necessary for marriage to make a great deal of difference to a man's life. He was expected to provide generous marriage settlements; beget, if possible, heirs to his estates and fortune; and appear with his wife on all appropriate social occasions. Otherwise they were free to go their separate ways.

Nor was it that he disliked women, or they him. Vivyan, whose adolescent hero-worship of his soldier cousin had deepened since Greydon left the army into a strong and comfortable friendship, wondered sometimes just what quality Grey possessed to attract women of such widely differing types as (for instance) the modest and well-bred Miss Marstow and the dashing Cyprian who was currently enjoying his protection. The cynical would say it was his great wealth; Vivyan did not believe this was the only reason. Yet the attraction could scarcely be supposed to lie in his looks, for though he possessed an undeniably splendid physique, his features bore little resemblance to the popular conception of a handsome man, being of an aquiline cast, and a naturally olive complexion which his years of soldiering had darkened to a gipsy swarthiness. He had eyes of a brown so dark that it seemed almost black, deep-set below black brows that slanted upwards, thick and strongly marked; lean cheeks and a strong, determined jaw. It was a face which had seemed old for its years at twenty, had aged very little in the ten years since then, and would probably look much the same at fifty, or even sixty. Not, one would imagine, a face to set female hearts fluttering, and yet flutter they undoubtedly did.

'Blue-devilled, Grey?' Vivyan suggested tentatively at length.

'Something more than that,' Sir Greydon admitted. He hesitated, but then appeared to come to a sudden decision. 'Oh, the devil! Since you are here I may as well tell you, for God knows how much longer I can keep the matter secret. The reason I came so hurriedly to Rushbourne, Viv, and why I am still here, is that the Medallion has been stolen.'

* * *

Vivyan's eyes widened, and he stared at his cousin in shocked disbelief; after a moment he said uncertainly:

'You cannot be serious!' Then, immediately correcting himself: 'Of course you are! You would not say that in jest. My God, Grey, what a thing to happen! Does anyone else know?'

'Only Mayhew, for it was he who discovered the theft. As my agent he holds a key to the strong-room, where, as you know, the Medallion was kept in its iron casket. I have one of the only two keys to that—the other is lodged with my lawyer—and on the last occasion that

Mayhew visited the strong-room he found that the casket had been forced open and the Medallion removed. He came at once to me, and naturally I lost no time in getting here.' He paused, and then added with grim meaning: 'You perceive that I could give no adequate reason for my abrupt departure, least of all to our grandmother.'

'No, by God!' Vivyan agreed. 'Grey, if she knew—if she found out—!'

'It would almost certainly kill her,' Greydon concluded as Vivyan hesitated. 'You know how implicitly she believes in the legend.'

'Can't really wonder at that, I suppose,' Vivyan said reluctantly. 'Not after what happened.'

Sir Greydon agreed, though with a touch of impatience. The Varleigh Medallion was the family's most treasured heirloom, a massive circle of pure gold, strangely wrought and set with precious stones. It had been brought to England by that Elizabethan seafarer who founded the family fortune, and the tale which had been passed from generation to generation was that it had been bestowed upon him by an Aztec prince whose life he had saved. Whether this were true, or whether the Medallion was merely one of the prizes of a piratical affray against Spain, would never now be known, but it was indisputable that the earlier Sir Greydon had regarded the Medallion as the source of the great good fortune which followed his acquisition of it. On his death-bed he had warned that it must never upon any account be removed from the Abbey, or disaster would follow; his heir believed him and laid a similar command upon his own son, and so a tradition and a legend had been born. The Varleigh Medallion was synonymous with the Varleigh luck, and if the old sea-dog's more sceptical descendants regarded this as no more than a quaint, archaic superstition they had nevertheless, with one notable exception, abided by it. The exception was Sir Andrew Varleigh, the grandfather of Greydon and Vivyan, who on one occasion had taken the Medallion to his London house. It could have been only a tragic coincidence that, within a week, Sir Andrew's only son, his wife, and the elder of their two little boys died in an accident, but the tragedy convinced Lady Varleigh of the truth of the legend, and that conviction had never wavered. Even Sir Andrew's scepticism had been shaken. The Medallion was returned with all speed to its rightful place and had never again left it. Never—until now.

'Wait a minute!' Vivyan had been thinking over what Greydon had told him, and now perceived something odd. 'You said that the casket had been forced open, but what about the door of the strong-room?'

'That had been opened with a key. I should have explained that to you, and also that, besides the Medallion, a very considerable sum of money is missing.' Sir Greydon paused, and the added in his driest tone: 'And so is Cousin Oliver.'

'Well, I'm damned!' Vivyan said softly. 'Mind you, I never liked the fellow, but I would not have supposed—wait, though! Didn't you and he have a turn-up some time last winter?'

'We did.' Greydon agreed rather grimly. 'It had been brewing for a long time, ever since I sold out, and it finally came to a head.'

Mr Calderwood nodded wisely. 'I'm not surprised. Thought last time I was here that you'd not be able to endure his insolence for much longer. In your place, I'd have drawn his cork long since.' He added hopefully: 'Did it come to that?'

'I am ashamed to admit that it did. It was a sordid business altogether, concerning an unfortunate girl in the village, hardly more than a child herself. I told Oliver to his head that I had had a surfeit of his scoundrelly conduct, and that unless he mended his ways he would leave Rushbourne for good. I will admit that I did not spare his feelings, but it was really very foolish of him to try to plant me a facer.'

'Suicidal, I should call it,' Vivyan retorted with a fleeting grin, for Sir Greydon was known in sporting circles as a first-rate amateur pugilist. 'Oh well, it was bound to happen sooner or later. Thought so for a long time.'

'Perhaps, but it is not an incident in which I take any pride. For one thing, Oliver is nearly ten years older than I and by no means up to my weight, and for another, his circumstances are devilish difficult, and have been from the day he was born.'

'I'd say he has been damned fortunate all his life, thanks to Grandfather.'

'Would you?' Greydon spoke reflectively. 'I wonder. It's true he has been adequately provided for, but there *are* other considerations to take into account. You know, Viv, as a child I detested Oliver, but when I grew old enough to appreciate how equivocal his situation is, I began to feel sorry for him.'

'I'll lay odds he don't appreciate your sympathy.'

'Good God, no! Had he ever suspected it, which I trust he never did, he would have resented it bitterly. Just as he has always resented me.'

'Queer thing, that!' Vivyan observed. 'I mean, why *should* he resent you? It's not as though you had cut him out of the inheritance, or anything of that kind. He has no rights at Rushbourne.'

'Precisely! He has lived here on sufferance all his life, simply because of Grandfather's affection for Great Aunt Olivia, and he has never been able to forget that. He resented me because I was the heir, just as I am sure he would have resented my brother had he lived. One cannot blame him. It is a damnable situation to be in.'

'I suppose so,' Vivyan agreed soberly. 'Can't say I had ever considered it before, but I can see that you are right.'

They were silent for a while, each contemplating the unenviable situation of Cousin Oliver. He was the son of Olivia Varleigh, who forty years before had celebrated her seventeenth birthday by eloping with a plausible rogue whose company had been strictly forbidden to her. Of all her outraged family only her half-brother, Sir Andrew, twenty years her senior and looking upon her as a daughter rather than a sister, was prepared to stand by her, and instead of utterly disowning her and expunging her name from the family records, at once caused a search to be made. Since he was her legal guardian no one could gainsay him, even when the affair turned out to be even more scandalous than had first been supposed. A month elapsed before the fugitives were found—or rather, before Olivia was found, for the man, getting wind of the pursuit, abandoned her and fled for his life—and it was left to Sir Andrew to break the news that the wedding ceremony she had gone through meant nothing, since the 'bridegroom' already had a wife.

In the face of family disapproval he brought her home to Rushbourne, and when her child was born it was given the name of Oliver Varleigh and placed in the nursery with Sir Andrew's own youngest children, tolerated but never accepted by Sir Andrew's wife. Olivia died while her son was still in leading-strings, but the boy continued to be brought up with his cousins; educated, though not at the same school as Sir Andrew's sons; and finally provided with a modest income from that portion of the Varleigh fortune which had been set aside for his mother, who in looks he greatly resembled. It was unfortunate that in all other respects he took after his unprincipled father.

'What a devilish thing to happen!' Vivyan remarked at length. 'Grey, what are you going to do?'

'It has been difficult to know *what* to do,' Greydon replied bitterly. 'The whole damnable business must be kept secret if possible, for apart from the danger of Grandmama getting wind of the theft, you can imagine with what glee the scandalmongers would seize upon so unsavoury a morsel, and that, to a great extent, has tied my hands. Add to that the fact that Oliver has completely disappeared, and you will begin to appreciate the quandary in which I find myself.'

'You mean he has made off? Well, he would, wouldn't he?'

'I mean that he has disappeared, literally without trace. He left Rushbourne on the morning after the theft, telling the servants he expected to be away for several days, and has not been seen since.'

Vivyan frowned. 'How do you know precisely when the theft took place?'

'By merest chance. Oliver must have been planning it for some while, for he chose a moment when he might expect it to go undiscovered for a considerable time. You know that at this time of year Mayhew makes his round of annual visits to the other properties, and I would not expect to visit Rushbourne during the Season. Mayhew did in fact set out, as Oliver must have known he intended to do, but had gone only a mile or two on his way when he realized that certain documents he needed had been left behind in the strong-room. He came back for them, and discovered what had happened.'

'Curst ill luck for Oliver! How long would it have gone undiscovered if Mayhew had not forgotten those papers?'

'Oh, a fortnight at least! He would ordinarily be away that long, and I had no intention of coming here before the end of the Season.'

'Oliver's a damned cool customer, isn't he?' Vivyan remarked with grudging admiration. 'Fancy riding off from Rushbourne with the Medallion in his pocket.'

'Scarcely that, I imagine. After all, it is six inches across and proportionately heavy. One can only assume that he committed the theft during the night, concealed the proceeds somewhere away from the house, and collected them again next day. As you say, a cool customer!'

'And you can find no trace of him at all?'

'None whatsoever. Of course, I have been able to make only the most discreet inquiries, but I must have visited almost every inn and posting-house within a score of miles. I know that he was riding that evil-tempered grey, but no one seems to recall seeing him, neither has his horse been left at livery anywhere that I can discover.' He picked up the decanter again and filled both Vivyan's glass and his own. 'Now I suppose I have no choice but to do what I should perhaps have done in the first place. Call in the Runners.'

'Bow Street?' Vivyan was startled. 'Grey, won't that kick up the devil of a dust?'

'Very probably, which is why I had hoped to settle the

whole confounded business myself, but I dare not delay much longer if there is to be any hope at all of finding Oliver before he disposes of the Medallion.'

'He'd not be able to sell it, surely?'

'Only for a fraction of its real value. My greatest fear is that he may have it broken up, the jewels prised from their setting to be sold separately, and the gold melted down. He could make more profit that way, with less danger to himself.'

'Yes, by God! Grey, that may already have been done.'

'I think not. He would have to find a goldsmith whom he could trust to keep any suspicions to himself, and that would be impossible in a country district. I suspect that he has gone to London.'

'He would be safer out of the country.'

'Yes, but remember that Oliver has never travelled abroad, and speaks no language but his own. I do not think he will attempt to leave England until he has disposed of the Medallion, and he need be in no great haste to do that. As I told you, he stole a large sum of money as well, so he is not pressed for funds.'

'Damned scoundrel!' Vivyan said angrily. 'Make what excuses you like for him, Grey, the fact remains that he knows what store Grandmama sets by that confounded bauble, and how the theft of it must distress her.'

'Precisely, but that is not likely to trouble Oliver. There is no love lost there.' Greydon's voice held a note which warned Vivyan not to pursue that train of thought. 'Viv, are you willing to help me in this matter?'

'Of course I am. Dash it all, Grey, you've no need to ask that!'

'I beg your pardon. The thing is that though I decided today that I must call in the Runners, I am very reluctant to return to London at present, particularly in view of what you tell me of Grandmama's frame of mind. I thought of sending Stubbs with a letter, but it would be far better if you would go to Bow Street for me—with my authorization, of course.'

'I'll do it,' Vivyan agreed promptly, 'but it seems to me that any trail Oliver may have left will be cold by now.'

'Job's comforter!' Greydon retorted wryly. 'I fancy that Bow Street has sources of information denied to the ordinary citizen, and if an article as rare and as valuable as the Medallion has made an appearance in London, there are bound to be rumours of it among the criminal fraternity. That, at least, must be our hope.'

Vivyan nodded. 'I'll set off first thing in the morning.'

'No,' Greydon said quickly. 'For one thing, I would not be so ungrateful as to expect that of you, and for another, it would present a very odd appearance if you were to stay only one night after coming expressly to visit me. It may not be possible in the end to keep this unsavoury business secret, but for the present I intend to use every means in my power to do so.'

'Whatever you say,' Mr Calderwood agreed amicably. 'I shall have to try to think of some tale which will satisfy Grandmama, and the longer I have to do that, the better!'

Part 3

To the relief of his mother and sisters, Theodore suffered no serious consequences of his adventure. Dr Bamfield, who came promptly in answer to the summons—a promptness, Dione suspected, due largely to the fact that the visit was made at Sir Greydon Varleigh's request—advised a couple of days in bed as a precaution, but dismissed with gentle scorn Mrs Mallory's tearful declaration that never again should Theo be allowed to roam alone about the countryside. The doctor, a stocky, middle-aged man with grizzled hair and a kindly, blunt-featured face, had achieved something of a miracle by establishing at once a cordial relationship with his patient, who in spite, or perhaps because of his many encounters with doctors, was apt to be antagonistic towards the medical profession.

'Nonsense, my dear lady!' Dr Bamfield said cheerily to Mrs Mallory. 'Your son is not robust, I know, but you will not help him by treating him always as an invalid. Due care, of course, and escapades like this one best avoided, but I can see no reason why he should not outgrow a great deal of his delicacy as time goes by.'

Mrs Mallory was dubious, but Dione, who for some time had privately held the belief that Theodore would do better with less of the anxious cosseting lavished upon him by his mother and Aunt Winton, was in wholehearted agreement, and found in Dr Bamfield yet another assurance that the move to Garth House would prove to be of benefit to her brother.

Theodore's kindly feelings towards his doctor suffered a setback when, the next day proving to be warm and sunny, he found that neither cajoling nor sulking could prevail upon his mother to allow him to get up. In vain he declared that he felt perfectly well; Mrs Mallory, so persuadable in most matters, could be adamant where Theodore's wellbeing was concerned, and the only concession she would make was to carry her sewing to his room in order to keep him company. Dione, appealed to, showed less than her usual sympathy, saying briefly that he was a tiresome little boy, and that being confined to bed on a beautiful day was no more than he deserved for giving them all such a fright.

Dione, in fact, though she took care not to betray it, was herself suffering from reaction from the events of the previous evening, her muscles stiff and aching from the climb up the hill, following as it had a hard day's work in the house. The prospect of more housework was uninviting, but she had an uneasy suspicion that if none was done that day, they would all find it difficult to bring themselves to start again. Only the hall, she told herself wearily. Once that was made presentable, all the unused rooms could remain shut, the dust and decay within ignored for the time being.

Once they had started, however, even Dione was daunted by the magnitude of the task. Unlike the other rooms, the ceiling in the hall was high, accommodating as it did the staircase and the gallery, and the cobwebs which hung there in dark festoons were out of reach even of the broom which she tied to the end of a long pole. Nor were matters improved by the clouds of dust resulting from Ibstone's bad-tempered assault on the huge fireplace. Ibstone himself, as soon as the piles of ash had been removed, beat a retreat to some apparently urgent task in the kitchen garden, and his daughter, too, would have made her escape had Dione granted her an opportunity. Frustrated in this, Molly worked in a deliberately slap-dash way, complaining until Dione's fingers itched to box her ears. She knew that the girl was hoping to be sent back to the kitchen, but though she was of very little help. Dione was grimly determined not to allow her to escape.

Molly, however, was to have her revenge. She was standing on a step-ladder, desultorily cleaning one of the windows flanking the front door, while Dione polished the massive oak table in the centre of the hall. Edwina, on her knees, was busy with the legs of the same table, and Cecilia, who had undertaken the laborious task of cleaning the ornately carved balustrade of the gallery and staircase, was seated on a stair halfway down the topmost flight. Suddenly Molly descended the ladder with more energy than she had yet shown, and as she reached the floor a brisk knocking sounded upon the front door. Dione jumped, but before she could issue any instruction Molly had flung the door wide in a welcoming manner, revealing two immaculately attired gentlemen on the threshold.

'It be Sir Greydon Varleigh,' she announced unnecessarily, with a smirk of malicious satisfaction, 'and another gentleman.'

Sir Greydon and Dione stared at each other in almost equal dismay. He had seen the grin on Molly's face as she opened the door, realized that she was prompted by spite and not by ignorance, and that his arrival could scarcely have been more inopportune. Dione, robbed of any chance of retreat, could think only, with stunned horror, of the spectacle she and her sisters must present, and that she must now receive these exceedingly fashionable visitors attired in her oldest gown, a capacious apron and a remarkably unbecoming mob-cap which completely concealed her hair. Edwina, still kneeling, seemed to be endeavouring to hide under the table, while a quick glance at the stairs showed that Cecilia, cravenly, had fled. With the calmness of despair, Dione went forward to greet her guests.

'Thank you, Molly. Pray tell Mrs Mallory that Sir Greydon has called. You will find her in Master Theo's room.' She held out her hand. 'It is good of you to visit us, sir, and I am glad of this opportunity to thank you for sending Dr Bamfield to us so promptly.'

Sir Greydon had never before found himself calling upon a lady who was busy cleaning her house, nor could he imagine any other lady of his acquaintance being surprised in such a situation, but if they were, he thought with sudden admiration, not one of them could have carried it off with more aplomb than Miss Mallory was doing. So instead of apologizing for his intrusion he shook the rather grubby hand extended to him, replied in a similar vein, and begged leave to present his cousin, Mr Calderwood.

Dione, slightly comforted by his manner, and even more by the friendly smile which accompanied his words, made Mr Calderwood welcome, and begged the gentlemen to step into the parlour, adding to her youngest sister, still on her knees:

'Get up, Edwina, and make your curtsy. Our guests will forgive us for receiving them in this fashion, but they will think it excessively odd if you hide from them under the table.'

Edwina, too young to disguise her embarrassment as Dione was doing, continued to kneel, scarlet-cheeked and close to tears, until Vivyan, whose astonishment could not overcome an innate good nature, stretched down a hand to her and said with a grin:

'Cramp, eh, Miss Edwina? Deuced uncomfortable thing to happen. Let me help you up.'

Edwina, shyly obeying, found herself heaved to her feet by a tall, handsome and smiling young gentleman, and immediately fell in love with him with all the promptness and thoroughness of her fourteen years. This had the effect of making her blush more than ever, curtsy in tongue-tied silence, and trail behind them to the parlour, where she established herself in a corner and gazed adoringly at Mr Calderwood for the remainder of his visit.

Dione, meanwhile, recklessly deciding that tousled

hair was preferable to that hideous mob-cap, had pulled off the offending article as they crossed the hall and stuffed it into her apron pocket. In the parlour, she invited the gentlemen to be seated, and assured them that her mother would join them in a few minutes.

'I believe you said, ma'am,' Sir Greydon remarked, 'that Mrs Mallory is with your brother. I trust this does not mean that he has suffered any ill effects from his ducking?'

Dione laughed. 'Not in the least, sir, I am happy to say, but Dr Bamfield advised keeping him in bed for a day or two. This was not well received in such fine weather, and my mother has tried to soften the blow by sitting with him. I fear, though, that news of your arrival will make it even more difficult for him to reconcile himself, for he has talked of nothing but your horses ever since he woke up.'

'Horse mad, is he?' Vivyan said sympathetically. 'I was the same at that age.'

'Yes, and very tiresome you were,' Sir Greydon informed him, 'which is why I am able to sympathize with Miss Mallory. I must beg your forgiveness, ma'am. There are few things more wearisome than a small boy's obsession with some pet subject, even when one is an enthusiast oneself.'

'Well, *I* admire fine horses,' Dione admitted, 'but I am lamentably ignorant about them. Theo, on the other hand, contrived to acquire a certain amount of knowledge in my aunt's stables when we lived in London, and is inclined to despise the rest of us for not sharing it. Perhaps it is just as well he is confined to bed, for I fear he would have found such an opportunity too good to miss, and would have pestered you with interminable questions.'

'We would have left my cousin to answer them, ma'am. That would have been a fitting revenge for the questions he was used to inflict upon me.'

This made Dione chuckle, and Sir Greydon reflected again that hers was the most unaffected feminine laughter he had ever heard. He was conscious of a growing curiosity about the Mallory family, and why, however indigent their circumstances, they had not taken one horrified look at Theodore's inheritance and then returned forthwith to London. That they intended to stay was obvious from the attempt which was being made to furbish up the house; he had no need to speculate as to who was the instigator of that endeavour, and found her determination to make a home out of this decaying ruin both funny and touching.

Mrs Mallory came fluttering into the room, with breathless greetings, and apologies for Cecilia, who had remained upstairs with her brother, to make certain that he stayed in bed.

'For as soon as he learned that you, Sir Greydon, had called, he wanted to get up, and come and thank you for your kindness last night. At least,' she added doubtfully, 'that is what he said, and I am sure I hope he meant it, though I very much fear that what he really wanted to talk about is horses.'

Vivyan, who had come hoping to make the acquaintance of the pretty blonde sister, was disappointed, but Dione and Sir Greydon exchanged a glance of mutual appreciation and amusement. To Mrs Mallory, Greydon said:

'I am happy to hear that he is so much recovered, ma'am. I will confess that I was a trifle concerned last night, and felt that I must come to see how he goes on.'

The widow smiled warmly at him, and thanked him in earnest tones for his solicitude. 'Such a comfort, Sir Greydon, to encounter kindness when one is a stranger, for though my late husband was Mr Jonathan Mallory's nearest relative, we were scarcely acquainted. I dare say you knew Mr Jonathan better than I.'

Sir Greydon shook his head. 'I think not, ma'am. I remember him, of course, from my childhood, but he was elderly even then. All I can recollect about him is that he was slightly lame and always leaned upon a stick. I entered the army as soon as my education was completed and was scarcely at Rushbourne at all until after the war ended, and by that time Mr Mallory was so advanced in years that he never left Garth House.'

'Yes, he was nearly ninety-two when he died, I am

told, and I greatly fear that he was not very well looked after in his latter years. One cannot help feeling a trifle guilty, for though our relationship was not close, we are the only family he had, and I should perhaps have used greater endeavours to communicate with him. Perhaps even removed here, so that we could look after him.'

Sir Greydon and Vivyan, who, though too young to have been acquainted with Jonathan Mallory, had heard enough about the old gentleman to guess how such a proposal would have been received, exchanged a pregnant glance. Dione, intercepting this, felt a stab of curiosity, but since this was not the time to indulge it, she said briskly:

'Well, I am sure we should have been very happy to do so, and one thing at least is certain. If we *had* been here, the house would not have been allowed to fall into such dirt and disorder. Though I do not think, Mama, that you have any cause to reproach yourself. If Cousin Jonathan had wished to trace us he could have done so, as his lawyer contrived to do after his death, so we can only conclude that he did *not* wish to make our acquaintance.'

This commonsense point of view (which Sir Greydon felt certain was characteristic of Miss Mallory) did not seem altogether to satisfy her mother, but she did not pursue the matter. The conversation turned to more general topics, and after some twenty minutes the gentlemen took their leave. Mrs Mallory herself escorted them to the door, explaining, when she returned to the parlour, that she would not have trusted Molly to show them out, after what had happened on their arrival.

'How *could* she be so stupid as to admit visitors to the house without first giving you a chance to withdraw?' she lamented. 'I hope you will take her severely to task, Dee!'

'I shall do nothing of the kind. That was not stupidity, Mama! It was downright malice, because I had kept her hard at work all the morning. She wished to put me in an uncomfortable situation and she succeeded, but I shall not give her the added satisfaction of laughing at me in her sleeve while I scold her for it.'

'But to be obliged to receive two gentlemen of fashion dressed like that! When Cecy came running to tell me, I was ready to sink.'

'*You* were ready to sink, Mama?' Dione retorted with some indignation. 'What do you suppose my feelings were? If I could have rendered myself invisible I would gladly have done so.'

'Dee was splendid!' Edwina said admiringly, emerging at last from the trance-like state induced by her meeting with Mr Calderwood. 'She behaved just as she would have done if she had been wearing her best gown, and—and playing the pianoforte instead of polishing the furniture.'

'It seemed the only thing to do,' Dione admitted. 'Fortunately, Sir Greydon is too great a gentleman to betray the astonishment and disgust he must have felt, and both he and Mr Calderwood exerted themselves to put us at our ease, but I hope never to have to endure such embarrassment again.'

'I still think,' Mrs Mallory objected, 'that Molly ought to be punished for doing such a thing.'

'She will be, Mama!' Dione pulled the mob-cap from her pocket and crammed it on, pushing her hair up beneath it with a determined air. 'I am going to set her to work again at once, and this time we are not going to stop until the hall is as clean as we can possibly make it. That will be a far worse punishment to Molly than any amount of scolding.'

* * *

Their next encounter with Sir Greydon Varleigh took place the following Sunday. The question of attending church had greatly exercised Mrs Mallory's mind, for the village was half a mile away and Garth House could provide no means of transport except the rough cart and ancient horse used by Ibstone for marketing and similar tasks. Dione, appealed to, said calmly that if it were fine, they would walk; if not, they would be obliged to stay at home and make do with family prayers.

Fortunately for Mrs Mallory's peace of mind—for she would have considered it very wrong not to attend a church service each Sunday—the day proved fine and warm, with just enough breeze to temper the heat of the sun. They set out in time to walk at a leisurely pace, and reached the church while the rest of the congregation were going in. There were several carriages in the avenue leading to the churchyard, and Mrs Mallory and her family felt themselves to be the cynosure of attention, though no one spoke to them except a churchwarden, who indicated which was the Garth House pew, thus indicating also that their identity was known to the inhabitants of Brambledon.

After the service, however, the Vicar made a point of speaking with them as they were leaving the church, welcoming them to the parish and saying how happy he was to see the Garth House pew occupied again, since for a number of years Mr Jonathan Mallory's great age had prevented him from attending services. Mrs Mallory made some suitable reply and presented her children, and they went out into the sunshine feeling not quite such outsiders as when they arrived.

This comforting sensation, however, was rapidly dispelled by the stares, ranging from curious to frankly disparaging, which were directed towards them. One formidable matron in particular, very fashionably dressed and with two rather plain but equally fashionable young ladies accompanying her, subjected them to a haughty scrutiny which missed no detail of their simple, home-made gowns and their shoes dusty from their walk to church. She then made some inaudible but obviously scornful remark to the younger women and turned away, blocking, by accident or design, the way through the gate between churchyard and avenue.

Mrs Mallory hesitated, waiting for her to move, and was ignored; a timid request to pass fell upon (apparently) deaf ears; and Dione, her temper rising, was about to intervene when a man's firm step sounded on the path beside her, and Sir Greydon's voice addressed her mother by name.

Mrs Mallory turned, and so, quickly, did the haughty matron and her daughters, but Sir Greydon, greeting first Mrs Mallory and then Dione and her sisters, seemed as blind as they had previously appeared deaf. Finally he glanced at Theodore.

'So you have been released from durance, Theo? I trust you have undertaken no more voyages of discovery?'

'No, sir, and I never properly thanked you for helping me that evening. I—I am excessively obliged to you.' Theodore paused, seemed to struggle briefly with himself, and then added in a triumphant whisper: 'You see, Dee? I never said a word about horses.'

Mrs Mallory shook her head sadly, Dione bit back a chuckle, and Sir Greydon said, with only the faintest quiver of amusement in his voice:

'Stubbs is in the avenue with my curricle. It occurs to me, Theo, that if your mama permits, you may care to look at the horses, and to talk to him about them.'

Theodore, barely waiting for his mother's approval, slid nimbly past the three ladies in the gateway and hurried away, while Sir Greydon, apparently becoming aware of their presence at last, added easily:

'Mrs Elverbury, how charming to see you! Your servant, ma'am. Miss Elverbury, Miss Clara.'

The greeting was returned, the lady as amiable now as she had previously been frosty; her daughters simpered and blushed. Sir Greydon then begged leave to present Mrs Mallory, and if the other woman's cordiality faded a little, enough of it remained to enable her to respond civilly, and to remain so while the young ladies were made known to each other. Sir Greydon looked on with a faintly sardonic gleam in his eyes, while Dione, deeply appreciative of his social adroitness, but even more of the kindness which prompted it, bestowed upon him a look warm with gratitude. She had seen him come into church, and had expected no more than a civil bow if they encountered him after the service; instead he had gone out of his way to rescue them from embarrassment. For herself, Dione could have shrugged off Mrs Elverbury's disdain with no more than a passing discomfiture, but her mother and Cecilia were far more vulnerable and would have shrunk from running the gauntlet on future occasions. Dione was shrewd enough to realize that to be upon terms with Sir Greydon Varleigh was a sure passport to acceptance in Brambledon, and that others beside Mrs Elverbury would have remarked the encounter.

Such interested persons were to remark also that Sir Greydon, having handed Mrs Elverbury and her daughters into their carriage (which was awaiting, doubtless to that lady's annoyance, just outside the gate), strolled on with the newcomers until they reached his curricle, where Theodore was talking earnestly to Stubbs, and remained for several minutes in conversation with them. It was further noted that the fair-haired young lady from Garth House was exceptionally pretty, and assumed that this was the source of Sir Greydon's interest in the family. Few would have believed that he noticed Cecilia hardly at all.

* * *

Mrs Mallory was tired when they reached home, but in a happier frame of mind than she had known since their arrival. The solitude of Garth House, and its situation, seemingly cut off from the rest of the world, had weighed upon her more than she cared to admit, while the reception accorded them that day in the village had depressed her even more. Sir Greydon's courtesy and kindness had done much to restore her spirits, which had been raised even further when, after Varleigh had driven away, Dr Bamfield came up to them, introduced his wife and son (an inarticulate young man who gazed at Cecilia with unfeigned admiration) and stood chatting with them for several minutes. For the first time, Mrs Mallory began to feel that life in Brambledon might possibly be more than something to be endured for Theodore's sake.

Theodore himself was hugely elated because Sir

Greydon, hearing part of his conversation with Stubbs and recognizing the intelligent interest it betrayed, had promised to take him driving one day. Dione had raised her brows a little at this, for though she had never moved in fashionable circles, she guessed that Corinthians such as Sir Greydon Varleigh did not commonly indulge to this degree small boys who had no claim upon them, but Mrs Mallory saw nothing odd in this uncommon favouring of her son. Such a treat was, in her opinion, only what Theodore deserved.

Later that day, however, she felt almost inclined to agree with Dione that a treat was not what he deserved at all. The family, with the exception of Theodore himself, had gathered in the parlour just before dinner, and Molly was setting the table, when a slow, uneven footfall, accompanied by the measured tapping of a stick, was heard descending the stairs and crossing the flagstones of the hall. At first, Mrs Mallory and her daughters were merely puzzled, but then a strangled exclamation from Molly diverted their attention to her, and they saw that she was staring towards the door, her usually high colour quite gone and her eyes wide and horrified. Cecilia, always sensitive to the emotions of others, uttered a sound between a cry and a gasp and clutched Dione's arm; Mrs Mallory turned pale; and even Edwina, who was nearest to the door, retreated an involuntary pace. The sound drew nearer, and Dione, freeing herself from her sister's hold, stepped quickly forward and threw open the door. Just outside stood Theodore, leaning on a walking stick.

'Look what I found upstairs,' he greeted her. 'It must have belonged to Cousin Jonathan. Edwina told me Sir Greydon said that he was lame, and always walked with a stick.'

'This is a very stupid thing to do,' Dione informed him severely. 'We wondered who in the world could have got into the house, and it gave poor Molly quite a fright.'

Theodore came into the room, looking from one to the other. His mother and sisters were regarding him with varying degrees of exasperation, but Molly was still pale, and her hands as she arranged cutlery and plates on the table were shaking. A look of mischief came into Theodore's face.

'She thought I was a ghost! Cousin Jonathan's ghost,' he exclaimed delightedly. 'You did, Molly, didn't you?'

'That I never did, Master Theo,' she exclaimed indignantly. 'Not but what it gave me a turn, mind you, hearing you like that. You did sound for all the world like old Mr Mallory.'

'And he's dead, so you must have thought I was a ghost,' he said triumphantly. 'I didn't *mean* to frighten you, though. Dee, listen! It's the noise I heard, the one that woke me.'

'What noise, Theo?' Dione asked resignedly.

'This one!' He took a few paces forward, halting with one foot and leaning heavily on the stick. 'I found the stick and tried walking with it, and then I knew. That's what I heard, the first night we were here, and then again the next. That, and voices.'

She remembered his insistence at the time, but he had always been an imaginative child, inclined to confuse fact with fantasy, and she dismissed the thought after only a moment's consideration. It was an idea it might not be wise to encourage.

'If you heard voices at all, which I doubt, it could only have been those of Molly and her mother and father. Now stop it, Theo! You are trying to scare us, and will end by scaring yourself. We wish to hear no more of it, and of no more foolish pranks, either.'

He looked mutinous, but his mother, gently reproachful, added her voice to Dione's, while Dione herself took the stick from him and propped it in a corner of the room, bidding him take his seat at the dinner-table. He obeyed, and the matter was not referred to again. Dione hoped that it would be forgotten.

The following evening, however, an incident occurred which recalled it forcibly and unpleasantly to their minds. They were once again in the parlour, Cecilia helping Edwina with an intricate piece of sewing, while Dione and their mother discussed in low voices the propriety of sending a letter to Mrs Winton. Mrs Mallory, who disliked being upon bad terms with anyone, was of the opinion that she should write, but Dione was less enthusiastic.

'Of course you must do as you think best, Mama,' she said at length, 'but if you do write, do not, I beg of you, describe how we found matters here. It would be too humiliating, and—!'

'Listen!' Cecilia's voice, sharp with alarm, interrupted her. 'Mama, Dee, pray listen!'

Startled by her tone, and her sudden pallor, they obeyed, and heard again the halting steps and tapping stick, not in the hall this time, but on the floor above. For a moment even Dione was startled, but then she said wrathfully:

'Theo! The little wretch is at his tricks again. Say what you will, Mama, he will have to be punished!'

'It's not Theo,' Edwina said in an odd voice. 'I can see him in the garden. He went out to fetch his bat and ball.'

Dione was taken aback, but rallied almost immediately. Cecilia was looking terrified, and so was their mother.

'Then it must be Molly!'

'Dee!' Mrs Mallory protested. 'Why should Molly do such a thing?'

'To alarm us, of course, and from what I can see, she is succeeding admirably.'

She was on her way to the door as she spoke. Cecilia said faintly, 'Dee, no!' but an impatient glance was the only response. Dione went out, closed the door softly behind her and, catching up her skirts, ran lightly across the hall and up the stairs.

From the gallery it was possible to look left and right along the short corridors serving the upper rooms, and although the footsteps had now ceased, Dione expected to see Molly in the one above the parlour. To her surprise, this was empty, and so, as investigation proved were the rooms opening from it. Despising herself for feeling a twinge of alarm, she stood looking perplexedly about her until she remembered the back stairs. These were a steep spiral which stretched from attic to cellar and were entered, on the first floor, by a door at the end of the corridor in which she now stood. She went quickly and opened it, but felt no surprise at finding the stair deserted, for if Molly had gone that way she would have had ample time, accustomed as she must be to the twisting steps, to run quietly down to the kitchen.

'No,' Dione said in answer to the apprehensive looks which greeted her on her return to the parlour, 'I did not catch her. She must have run down the back stairs when she heard me coming up the front.'

'If it *was* Molly,' Cecilia retorted in a trembling voice.

'Of course it was Molly!' Dione said impatiently, 'Mama, you, at least, cannot seriously suppose anything else?'

'Good gracious, Dee, of course not!' Mrs Mallory replied, making a brave though not wholly successful attempt to speak with conviction. 'Come now, Cecy dear, there is no need to look so frightened. It must have been Molly, as your sister says.'

'Then it was a horrid thing to do!' Cecilia was almost in tears. 'I hope you will tell her so, Dee, and give her the most tremendous scold.'

'I shall do nothing of the kind,' Dione said flatly. 'That is just what she would like, for she would deny it, but know that she *had* alarmed us and made us look foolish. We shall say nothing at all about it.'

Reluctantly Cecilia agreed, but unfortunately it did not occur to Dione to forbid confiding in Theodore, and Edwina poured out the whole story to him as soon as he came into the room. He was reluctant to believe that Molly was responsible, but, far from being alarmed, was obviously much taken with the notion that Garth House might be haunted by the ghost of their aged relative. An apparition, it seemed, was the one thing needed to make his inheritance perfect in his eyes. He accepted without question Dione's command that Molly herself must not be challenged, but Dione suspected that this was largely because he did not want so mundane a suspicion to be confirmed.

* * *

She was thankful when, next day, her brother's thoughts were given a new direction by the arrival of Sir Greydon to take him for the promised drive, though she was secretly a little surprised that the casually given promise should be so promptly fulfilled. She was busy elsewhere in the house when the visitor arrived, and it was Mrs Mallory who received him and, a little later, waved goodbye from the front door as the curricle drove off, with Theodore, pale with excitement, seated between Sir Greydon and Stubbs. Greydon was disappointed, but concealed the fact and hoped for better fortune on his return.

The hope was fulfilled. When, an hour or so later, the curricle again drove up to Garth House, Dione was standing on the stretch of weed-grown gravel before the door. Ibstone was with her, and they were both looking up at the front of the house. It appeared to Sir Greydon that they were engaged in somewhat acrimonious argument, but as the carriage drew up, Miss Mallory said something with an air of finality and turned towards it, while Ibstone, with a surly look at the new arrivals, slouched off to the rear of the house, muttering audibly as he went.

Theodore, helped to the ground by Stubbs, raced towards his sister, bubbling over with an excited account of the treat he had been given. She listened indulgently until Sir Greydon strolled across to join them, and then broke in kindly but firmly, bidding her brother thank his benefactor and go into the house. It was time, she said, for him to get back to his school-books.

Sir Greydon, overhearing this, waited only until Theodore had conscientiously carried out the instructions before saying rather ruefully: 'Have I committed the solecism, ma'am, of interrupting his lessons? That should have occurred to me, of course, and I make you my apologies.'

She smiled and shook her head. 'There is no harm done, sir. It is only very recently that Theo has been well enough to do any lessons at all, and at present I set him no more than will occupy two or three hours a day. In any event, he was so greatly looking forward to driving with you that neither Mama nor I would have had the heart to deny him.'

He was regarding her with amusement not untouched by admiration. 'Are you responsible for your brother's education, Miss Mallory, along with everything else?'

'Only for the present,' she assured him quickly. 'My mother's old governess was used to live with us—Papa was in the navy, you understand—and we were all in turn taught by her. It was only when she died, a year ago, that I became responsible for teaching the younger ones. It will not serve for very long with Theo, of course, but he has been so much plagued by illness, poor little fellow, that he lags far behind the standard of education a boy of his age should have reached.'

'I apprehend that your father lost his life in the war, ma'am?'

'Yes, though not in battle. He died of a fever only a few months after Theo was born. Poor Mama! She was so proud and happy to have given him a son after three daughters—that is why she named him Theodore, the "gift of God"—but Papa never even saw him.' She was silent for a moment, and then added more briskly: 'Forgive me! I do not know why I am prosing on about family matters which can be of no possible interest to you.'

'On the contrary,' he replied promptly, 'I am guilty of an insatiable curiosity about my new neighbours.'

As he had hoped, this retort had the effect of banishing her brief melancholy, and calling forth the chuckle he found so delightful.

'That would be very flattering, Sir Greydon, if only I could believe it to be true.'

'I assure you that it is, though I am not so rag-mannered as to ask impertinent questions and must hope that you will let fall a crumb of information from time to time. I even refrained from questioning your young brother.'

'I would be astonished, sir, to learn that any questions were necessary. If I know Theo, he was only too ready to offer, unasked, all kinds of information, but for my own peace of mind I would prefer not to know what he said.'

'Nothing to put you to the blush, ma'am, I give you my word, though one thing he said has me in a puzzle. What is this nonsense about Garth House being haunted?'

Watching her, he saw the grey eyes cloud for a moment, but she only said lightly: 'Nonsense, sir, as you say. Theo himself played a silly trick, and I believe that put it into Molly's head to do the same. I was angry, because both Mama and Cecilia were frightened, but I judged it best not to tax Molly with it. She was bound to have denied it, and that would have alarmed them more than ever.'

His dark eyes quizzed her. 'The thought of a ghost does not alarm *you*, Miss Mallory?'

'It might, sir, if I believed in such things, but I dare say I have too little imagination. And even if such apparitions did exist, why in the world should we be troubled by that of a very old gentleman who no doubt died peacefully in his own bed?' A fleeting change in his expression stopped her short, and she added, between amusement and dismay: 'Do you mean to tell me that he did not?'

'I fear I must tell you so. Jonathan Mallory tripped on the stairs, and was killed by the fall.' He raised an inquiring eyebrow. 'Perhaps it would be as well if Mrs Mallory and Miss Cecilia did not know that?'

'Much the best,' Dione agreed firmly, 'though for my part I am not altogether sorry to know. I occupy Cousin Jonathan's room now, and it has more than once crossed my mind, usually just as I am climbing into bed, that he very likely died there. It is quite a relief to know that he did not.'

She thought, belatedly, that this sounded shockingly heartless, and cast a slightly anxious glance at Sir Greydon, only to find that he was trying not to laugh. He said, rather unsteadily:

'Even though you do not believe in ghosts, Miss Mallory?'

She made a little grimace. 'Quite absurd, is it not? I did not even know Cousin Jonathan, any more than I knew any of the other people who must have died in that bed, which is *centuries* old. How inconsistent one's feelings can be!'

'Most illogical,' he agreed with a smile. 'Tell me, why do you suppose Molly Ibstone would play such a trick upon you?'

'Oh, just to be disagreeable! She and her parents have made it very clear that they dislike us, and resent our coming here. I believe they have had matters so much their own way for so long that they have come to look upon Garth House as their own.'

'Very likely. Jack Ibstone is a complete ne'er-do-well, too idle to provide for his family, and I am told they were homeless and destitute when Mallory took them in. Mrs Ibstone was a servant here before her marriage, and perhaps he felt a responsibility towards her. As you say, they have had things pretty much their own way for years.'

'Well, they are not having their own way now,' she declared. 'They are the most disobliging creatures, and you cannot imagine the complaints and arguments I have had today simply because I desired Ibstone to cut back some of the wisteria from the doors and windows. It is quite disgraceful how the place has been allowed to go to rack and ruin, inside and out, but we shall set it to rights in time.'

He found her spirit admirable, and had not the heart to tell her that hard work and enthusiasm were not enough; that the whole ancient, crumbling fabric of the house needed skill and money lavished upon it if it were to survive. That realization must come one day, but he had no desire to be the one to deal the blow.

'It will be an uphill struggle, ma'am, if you hope to persuade Ibstone to pull his weight,' he said frankly. 'When you find you need more help than he is prepared to give, send word to Rushbourne, and I promise that you will get it.'

She smiled, but shook her head and said with finality:

'That is a kind thought, Sir Greydon, and I am grateful, but we could not possibly impose so upon your generosity. We shall contrive to make ourselves very comfortable here, I have no doubt. But you must think me shockingly ill-mannered to keep you standing out here. Will you not come into the house? I know Mama will wish to thank you for your kindness to Theo.'

He declined the invitation, adding that there was no need to thank him. He had enjoyed Theodore's company. Dione seemed amused.

'Well, I am sure it is very civil of you to say so,' she replied candidly. 'He *can* be engaging, but I find it difficult to believe, sir, that you are in the habit of entertaining children of his age, which makes it particularly kind in you to put yourself out for Theo's benefit. We are most grateful, though I cannot imagine why you should do it.'

'To fix my interest with *you*, Miss Mallory,' he replied promptly.

He had the satisfaction of knowing that he had startled her, for she gasped, and lifted a wide, incredulous gaze to meet his, but she recovered herself in a moment.

'Of course!' she agreed cordially. 'How foolish of me not to guess, for I can see how it is. You must have the greatest difficulty in establishing yourself in the eyes of any female.' She had recovered her countenance now, and the grey eyes laughed up at him without embarrassment. 'How very gullible you must think me, sir!'

He took the hand she had extended to him, and clasped it lightly for a moment, smiling down at her.

'I think you wholly enchanting,' he said, and bowed slightly, and left her, this time totally bereft of words.

* * *

It was just as well, Dione reflected, taking a somewhat agitated turn about the wilderness of garden, that he had left when he did, for she had not the slightest idea how she could or should have answered him. What in the world had prompted him to say such a thing? She was neither a debutante to be courted, nor a lady of fashion to be beguiled into an idle flirtation, and he was too kind a man, she felt sure, merely to amuse himself by flattering a woman in her situation with empty compliments. They were scarcely acquainted, and yet she had felt that a certain degree of friendship and understanding had already been established between them; she was comfortable with him—or had been until that extraordinary remark threw her into utter confusion. It was some time before she recovered her composure sufficiently to return to the house, and even then, although she was outwardly her usual calm and competent self, the 'why' of the incident continued to tease her. Only one explanation failed to occur to her—that he had spoken the simple truth.

Yet so it was. Sir Greydon Varleigh, that most eligible of bachelors, who had remained unmoved while the beauties of three London Seasons were paraded before him; who had been regretting for months the promise made to reassure an ailing old lady, but had resigned himself to the prospect of a fashionable marriage of duty and convenience, had found at last a woman who possessed all those hitherto indefinable qualities he had hoped for in a wife. He had been attracted to Dione Mallory at their first meeting, an attraction which had grown rapidly stronger with each subsequent encounter. Her directness, her gallant spirit, her ability to laugh at herself, all delighted him, and he was conscious of an urgent desire to lift from her all those cares and responsibilities which she shouldered so cheerfully. She was not beautiful; she probably lacked all those feminine accomplishments which fashion regarded as indispensable; his friends and relations would undoubtedly dismiss her as a mere penniless nobody; but he had fallen in love with her in a way he had never before experienced, and the sort of marriage he had previously contemplated was now unthinkable. It was as simple as that.

His inclination was to devote all his time and attention to her, but it was impossible to ignore the problem which had brought him to Rushbourne, and so to his meeting with Dione. Vivyan Calderwood had done his part in engaging the services of Bow Street, and a discreet individual had waited upon Sir Greydon at the Abbey to inform him that, in addition to inquiries being made in London, he had come to carry out an investigation on the spot. So far, neither effort had had any result. The whereabouts of Oliver Varleigh, and of the Varleigh Medallion, remained shrouded in mystery, and Sir Greydon was beginning to wonder whether it would ever be otherwise.

On the day after taking Theodore driving, he received two letters. One was from Vivyan, informing him that as far as Bow Street could discover, there was no whisper of a jewelled medallion being offered for sale in the underworld of London, and conveying the equally unwelcome news that Lady Varleigh was becoming increasingly out of charity with both her grandsons, the elder for his refusal to return to town, and the younger for his inability, which she regarded as deliberate prevarication, to offer any satisfactory explanation of his cousin's continued absence. Vivyan, Sir Greydon gathered from the harassed tone of his letter, was having a difficult time.

The second letter, written a day later, was from the Dowager herself, bitterly informing him that the engagement of Priscilla Marstow to the Earl of Riversdale had been announced, and that though she was deeply disappointed, for Miss Marstow was everything she had ever hoped for in a grand-daughter-in-law, she must remind him of the promise he had made to her almost a year ago (heavily underlined). He would oblige her by abandoning whatever preoccupation—probably disreputable, since he was so secretive about it—was keeping him at Rushbourne, and returning to town without delay. She had several other amiable and pretty-behaved young females in mind, any one of whom would make him a suitable wife.

None of this augured well for Dione, in the event of her returning his regard and accepting the offer of marriage he intended to make her. Lady Varleigh would certainly not regard Miss Mallory as a suitable wife for him, and it was difficult to decide which would be the greater shock to her; the announcement of such an engagement, or the theft of the Varleigh Medallion.

For the gloomy frame of mind engendered by the letters, there was only one remedy. Sir Greydon ordered his curricle, and drove to Garth House.

When he emerged from the drive, and the house came into view, he was surprised to see Dione, dressed in her Sunday best, standing on the front steps. Cecilia, in a plain, workaday gown, was with her, and Jack Ibstone, hands thrust deep into his pockets, stood before them in an attitude of complete indifference. Both sisters looked harassed, but at sight of the curricle Dione's expression brightened, and as Sir Greydon handed the reins to Stubbs and sprang down, she came quickly towards him, saying impetuously:

'If you have come to take Theo driving again, Sir Greydon, will you be so obliging as to take me instead?'

As he had known it would, her mere presence restored his good humour. He said with a smile:

'I can think of nothing more delightful, ma'am. Have you any preference as to where we shall go?'

She twinkled responsively back at him. 'As it happens, sir, I have. It is of the utmost importance that I go into town to see Mr Birkett, the lawyer, and Ibstone has been to the village to try to hire the innkeeper's gig, but by the greatest misfortune it is not to be had. Would it be asking too much of you to drive me there instead?'

'By no means, but you must forgive me for pointing out that it would be more proper for you to summon Birkett to wait upon you here.'

'Yes, I know.' She hesitated, and then moved a pace nearer, adding in a low voice: 'The thing is that if he came here, he would expect to deal with Mama, but I fear she has no head for business. Besides, she is never at ease with strangers, and is already distressed by the matter which has to be discussed with Mr Birkett. It would not do at all.'

He could well believe it, having realized that Mrs

Mallory was one of those shy, clinging females who were never able to fend for themselves. He wondered with some concern what problem had arisen, and wished that he had the right to inquire, but since he had not, the only thing he could do was to drive Dione to the town, and hope that she would choose to confide in him. He said soothingly that he perfectly understood, and with a bow to Cecilia handed Dione up into the curricle. He would have liked to dispense with Stubbs' presence in case she did wish to seek his advice, but he knew that even in a sleepy country town it would not do for her to be seen driving with him completely unattended. Not for the first time, he felt a surge of impatience at the petty restrictions imposed by the conventions of polite society.

Dione remained silent while they cautiously traversed the drive and then picked up to a brisker pace along the road. In her anxiety to get to town, and her relief at Sir Greydon's willingness to drive her there, she had forgotten how their previous meeting had ended, but now, remembering, she began to feel embarrassed. He had not meant it, of course. He had been merely jesting, but the fact remained that there was now a little awkwardness between them which had not been there before. Dione had had other admirers besides Eustace Winton, for her aunt, to do her justice, had always included her and Cecilia in any social occasion, but none of these worthies had belonged, as Sir Greydon did, to the world of fashion, where flirtation attained the level of an art. Such compliments as they paid her had been of a ponderous nature, and had tended to provoke her more to secret hilarity than anything else.

Sir Greydon, by no means inexperienced in the workings of the feminine mind, was able to hazard a tolerably accurate guess at the reason for her unaccustomed reserve, and exerted himself to win her out of it. As they approached the village, he solemnly drew her attention to the square Norman tower of the church, and recommended her, the next time she entered the sacred edifice, to take particular note of the remains of the medieval chancel-screen, which were thought to be especially fine. When she turned an astonished gaze upon him, he added reproachfully:

'Do not look so amazed, Miss Mallory. I am endeavouring to entertain you, in a quite unexceptionable way, by pointing out the more notable antiquities of our village. You will observe, for example, that the inn is an interesting timbered building of much the same period as Garth House—!'

'And in a far better state of repair,' she concluded ruefully. '*Is* there a medieval chancel-screen, sir?'

'Certainly there is. I have a vivid recollection of being invited to admire it, at an age when such things were of even less interest to me than they are now. If you wish to judge the depths of my indifference, point it out to Theodore the next time you take him to church.'

'Thank you, but I would as lief not do so. At present he has a tolerably good opinion of me, even going so far as to inform me that I am a "great gun", which I take to be praise of no mean order, and I do not wish to forfeit that. Which sets me in mind of something I wished to ask you. Theo has struck up a friendship with the boy who was bringing him home the night he fell into the pool. Is that an association which should be encouraged?'

'By no means—if you are so high in the instep that the thought of your brother on terms of friendship with a farmer's son offends you. If, on the other hand, you wish Theodore to have the companionship of an honest, trustworthy lad who will introduce him to some of the pleasures of a country boyhood—yes, indeed.'

'Exactly what I told Mama,' Dione observed with satisfaction. 'Poor Theo! What with indifferent health, and always having females about him, he has had a sadly dull time of it, yet he is by no means a milksop. It is the worst of bad luck that he has inherited his mama's delicate constitution.'

'And his eldest sister's spirit? I think he is very like you in character, if not in looks.'

'Yes, Theo and Edwina and I are all very much like Papa, except of course, that Theo takes his looks from Mama.'

'Do you remember your father, Miss Mallory?'

'Yes, though not very well, because he was so much away at sea. Cecilia has only a hazy recollection of him, and the two younger ones, of course, do not remember him at all. I have always felt that to be especially sad for Theo.'

'Very true. I lost both my parents, and my elder brother, when I was only five years old.'

'All at the same time? Oh, poor little boy!' Dione's eyes and voice were warm with compassion. 'How did so dreadful a thing happen?'

'They were travelling from London to Rushbourne when, some ten miles from here, they were overtaken by a violent thunderstorm. A tree beside the road was struck by lightning, the horses bolted, and the carriage overturned down a steep hillside. My mother and brother were killed outright, my father died shortly afterwards.'

'How very shocking, but what a mercy, sir, that you were not travelling with them!'

'Yes, my infant sister and I were suffering from some childish ailment, and had been left behind in London, with our nurse, in my grandmother's charge. We were fortunate, at least, in having devoted grandparents.'

'And your sister, sir?'

Oh, she is married now, and rarely leaves her husband's estate in Devonshire. She has four children—I think.'

'You *think*?' Dione repeated, laughing. 'Do you not know, sir?'

'It may be five.' He saw that in spite of her amusement she seemed a trifle shocked, and added in explanation: 'Elizabeth and I are not very closely acquainted, for you must remember that I was twelve years in the army, and in Spain for much of that time. She was in the schoolroom when I first joined my regiment, and a wife and mother by the time I sold out. We are sincerely attached to each other, but have very few interests in common.'

'No, I suppose not.' Dione's tone was reflective. 'No

doubt, being one of a very close-knit family, I cannot help finding that strange—though heaven knows why I should! Papa and Mr Jonahthan Mallory had not, as far as I know, any other close relations, and *they* only met two or three times in their lives. Mama wrote to Cousin Jonathan when she received news of Papa's death, but he never replied. Of course,' she added excusingly, 'he was very old, even then.'

Sir Greydon, recalling certain things he had heard about Jonathan Mallory, thought it likely that sheer selfishness and indifference, rather than the burden of his years, lay behind that gentleman's neglect of his kinsman's wife and children, but there seemed no point in saying so. He would have preferred to abandon the subject, but before he could introduce a new topic of conversation Dione went on:

'It may be, of course, that he was not then in a position to render Mama any assistance, and thought it best to hold no communication with her. His affairs must have been in a sad condition for a good many years, judging by the condition of his house, and I cannot help wondering why.'

She ended hopefully on a note of interrogation, and Greydon, after driving for a short distance in silence, said briefly:

'I have heard, ma'am, that Mr Mallory was a lifelong gambler. Not merely a *gamester*, you understand, but a man with an unfortunate predilection also for all kinds of speculation. That, I believe, is how a very respectable fortune dwindled away.'

She sighed. 'I suspected something of the kind. We knew, of course, that he had left very little money, but we had no notion of the deplorable condition of Garth House itself. Mama's recollection of it, from the only visit she ever made there, painted a very different picture.' She gave a rueful chuckle. 'The first hint *I* received that something might be amiss was the look that you, sir, gave me when I told you where to direct the post-boy. You had the appearance of one who could not believe he had heard aright.'

'I could not believe it. Had I been invited to hazard a guess as to which house in Brambledon was your destination, I would have named any in preference to Garth House. I was almost tempted to offer a word of warning, but felt it would be unwarrantable impertinence.' He glanced quizzically at her. 'Do you wish that I had?'

She gave the question some consideration, but finally shook her head. 'It would have made no difference, sir. We had no choice but to complete the journey.'

'And you intend to stay?'

'Most decidedly!'

There was a hint of defiance in the reply which he did not think was directed at him, and he wondered again what matter she had to discuss so urgently with the lawyer. He drove on in silence, to afford her an opportunity, if she desired one, to confide in him, but this time, it seemed, it was she who did not wish to pursue the subject. After a minute or two she asked some civil question about the countryside through which they were passing, and kept the conversation at that impersonal level until the town was reached.

Mr Birkett's place of business was in a tall, narrow house in the market-place. Dione, handed down from the curricle, was plainly expecting to go in alone, but this Sir Greydon would not permit.

'I shall see you safely into your lawyer's office, ma'am,' he said firmly, adding, more softly and with considerable amusement: 'And do not frown at me in that fashion, for it will make not the least difference.'

She looked as though she would like to make some retort, but that the street was too public a place to do so. Instead, with a speaking glance from those very expressive eyes, and a slightly exaggerated inclination of the head, she stepped through the door he was holding open for her into a narrow and rather musty passage. A second door gave access to an outer office where a couple of clerks were working; Sir Greydon stood aside to let Dione enter, and the younger of the two, seeing at first only a plainly dressed young woman requesting an interview with Mr Birkett, looked her over in a disparaging way and replied offhandedly that his employer was busy. Sir Greydon, unsurprised, stepped further into the room and said, quite pleasantly but with considerable authority:

'Miss Mallory has urgent business with Mr. Birkett. Pray be good enough to inform him immediately that she is here.'

The clerk, discovering that the young woman was escorted by what he later described to his cronies as an out-and-out swell, began to stammer excuses. He did not recognize Sir Greydon, but his colleague, a much older man, was better informed, and after a moment of stunned amazement, hurried forward to apologize, to offer the lady a seat, and to command his junior, in a meaning tone accompanied by a glare of such ferocity that the younger man positively quailed, to inform Mr Birkett that *Sir Greydon Varleigh* had brought Miss Mallory to see him. Impressed, the youth scurried away, to return almost immediately to invite the lady to step into Mr Birkett's private room.

Dione got up, directing a somewhat challenging glance at Sir Greydon, as though she expected him to insist upon accompanying her. He disarmed her by meeting her eyes with a look of understanding in his own, and saying with a slight smile:

'I will wait here for you to complete your business, Miss Mallory.'

Wait he did, declining the senior clerk's obsequious offer of a seat, and standing by the window with his back to the room, watching the comings and goings in the market-place, while behind him the clerks exchanged looks pregnant with unuttered questions and comments. He remained there until Miss Mallory emerged again, closing the door behind her with a decided snap; he turned then, regarded her thoughtfully for a moment, and then, nodding pleasantly to the other men, escorted her in silence from the room.

The two clerks looked at the closed door of their employer's sanctum, and then at each other; the younger raised his brows, the elder shrugged, and then both went back to their work, knowing that for once they were in total agreement. Mr Birkett was a woman-hating old curmudgeon who disliked and despised the entire female sex, but surely even he could have seen that a young woman who could keep the great Sir Greydon Varleigh kicking his heels in a dusty office for more than twenty minutes was worthy of more than ordinary consideration.

* * *

Sir Greydon had seen at a glance that his Dione was decidedly out of temper, for there was a becoming flush in her cheeks and her eyes were positively dark with anger. He made no comment; however, merely inquiring, as he handed her up into the curricle, if he might have the pleasure of providing her with some refreshment before they started on their return journey.

'Thank you, no,' she replied briefly. 'I am not in the least hungry or thirsty.'

He accepted this with a slight bow, but as he took his seat beside her and gathered up the reins, subjected her to a searching scrutiny of which, intent upon her own thoughts, she was unaware. While he drove out of the market-place and through the streets she sat in seething preoccupation, from which she was only roused by the carriage coming to a halt. Looking about, she found that he had left the town by a slightly different route and had drawn off the road on to a broad stretch of level turf under the branches of a row of elm trees. Beyond the trees was a grassy rise crowned by massive, ruined walls.

'What is it?' she asked. 'Why have we stopped here?'

'This is the castle from which the town derives its name. There is not a great deal of it left, but the view from what remains of the battlements is generally held to be the finest in the county.'

She stared at him. 'So it may be, sir, and I shall be happy to admire it—upon some other occasion.'

'Ah, but upon some other occasion the weather may

not be so favourable! Today is exceptionally clear, and you will be able to see every detail of a quite remarkable prospect.' He jumped down from the curricle and extended a compelling hand. 'I would not forgive myself, Miss Mallory, if I allowed you to forego it.'

Dione looked down at him with gathering wrath. He was smiling, but something in the dark eyes convinced her that he was prepared to wait indefinitely for her to comply. Had they been alone she would have argued, but in the presence of the groom, who had sprung down and gone to the horses' heads, an undignified wrangle was out of the question. In furious silence she allowed herself to be assisted to alight, placed her hand on Sir Greydon's proffered arm and walked with him between the trees and up the gentle slope beyond until they were out of earshot of the carriage. Then she halted and turned to face him.

'I am obliged to you, Sir Greydon, but you are well aware that at this present I have not the least desire to look at any view, however magnificent.'

'I know.' He took her hand, drew it firmly through the crook of his arm and held it there, compelling her to walk on with him. 'Whatever passed between you and Birkett has made you so angry that you can scarcely contain yourself, and I am persuaded that you would have found it quite impossible to complete the journey to Brambledon without giving vent to your vexation. To do so in front of Stubbs would be quite improper, and so I cast about in my mind for some opportunity for us to be private. The view from the castle seemed to me to meet the need admirably.' She made no response, and after a moment he added persuasively: 'Come now, Miss Mallory! I may be able to offer you advice or assistance, and even if I cannot, I will undertake to let you quarrel with me to relieve your feelings.'

If he had hoped that this last remark would win her to laughter he was disappointed, but after walking a few yards further in silence, she said in a voice tight with anger:

'That *odious* old man refused even to hold any

discussion with me. He had the—the *temerity* to inform me that females are incapable of comprehending any matter of business, and that it had been a grave error for us to take up residence at Garth House at all. We should have been guided, he said, by those wiser than we—meaning, of course, himself and Eustace Winton.'

With a heroic effort Sir Greydon preserved his gravity, though the picture her words conjured up of the scene which must have taken place in Mr Birkett's office was almost too much for him. When he was certain that he could control his voice he said sympathetically:

'I do not wonder that you are vexed, but—forgive my ignorance—who is Eustace Winton?'

'My cousin. At least,' she amended conscientiously, 'we call cousins, although there is no blood relationship. Mrs Winton is Mama's elder sister, and Eustace is her stepson.'

'Mrs Winton is the aunt with whom you were residing in London?'

Dione nodded. 'Yes. My aunt persuaded Mama to remove there five years ago, after Mr Winton died. She persuaded her that it would be best for Theo, though the truth was that she wished to have us all under her eye so that she could be sure we did only what *she* thought was proper.' She broke off, biting her lip. 'I should not have said that! My aunt was always generous to us, and it is true that in her house we enjoyed every comfort, but—!'

'But it galled you to be beholden to her,' he concluded as she hesitated. 'You dislike being under obligation to anyone, don't you, ma'am?'

She admitted it, a trifle ruefully, but added in self-justification: 'And Theo was *not* better, say what she would. In the end, the doctor informed Mama that his health would never improve while he lived in a large city, which is why she finally agreed to remove to Brambledon.'

That betraying use of the word 'finally' confirmed what he had suspected all along—that Dione had been the instigator of the enterprise, carrying her gentle, biddable Mama along on the tide of her own independence and enthusiasm. Equally certain, then, that the aunt had opposed the move; the only thing which remained shrouded in mystery was the crisis which had provoked today's visit to the lawyer.

'Am I to understand, ma'am,' he hazarded, 'that some difficulty has now arisen regarding your tenure of Garth House?'

She frowned. 'Not precisely. I mean, we have a perfect *right* to be there, for the property unquestionably belongs to Theo. What has been called in question is the *propriety* of our being there.' The recollection appeared to rouse her anger again. 'This morning, if you please, Mrs Ibstone received a note from Mr Birkett informing her that it is proposed either to sell Garth House, or to lease it to a tenant, and requesting her to compile a list of the most urgently needed repairs.'

'A formidable task,' he commented ironically, 'but are you telling me, Miss Mallory, that Birkett had the impertinence to apply to Mrs Ibstone rather than to your mother? That seems hardly believable.'

'Well,' she admitted rather guiltily, 'he can scarcely be blamed for that, for he did not know that we were there. I meant to inform him,' she continued hastily, 'but that did not seem nearly as urgent as making the house fit to live in. How was I to guess that Eustace would take it upon himself to write to him, without another word to *me*, informing him that it was to be either let or sold?'

They had reached the outworks of the castle now, and a fragment of ruined wall hid the curricle from the view. Greydon stopped and looked down at his companion.

'I assume,' he said severely, 'that Mr Eustace Winton, too, is unaware that you have removed there?'

She nodded, meeting his eyes with the beginning of a rueful twinkle in her own. 'He was absent from home when we left,' she confessed. 'The Wintons are bankers, and Eustace had travelled to the north on some matter of business. He wrote to Mr Birkett from there.'

'His stepmother had not informed him that you had left her house?'

The twinkle in Dione's eyes became more pronounced. 'My aunt's parting words,' she said demurely, 'were to the effect she washed her hands of us, and had no interest whatsoever in the disasters she was certain were about to befall us.'

'You did burn your bridges, didn't you?' he said with some amusement. 'I can see now why you have to make the best of Garth House.'

'No,' Dione said quickly. 'With all its faults, Garth House is to me far preferable to my aunt's home. It is our own, you see.'

'And do your mother and sisters agree with you?'

They were walking on now, and it was a moment or two before she replied. Then she said in a low voice:

'You mean, do you not, that I gave Mama no peace until she agreed to leave London? What a horrid, *managing* female you must think me!'

'I think,' he said gently, 'that you have been obliged to assume a great deal of responsibility, probably even while you were still in the schoolroom, and that your family have come to depend upon you to fight all their battles for them. They forget, perhaps, that the most ardent spirit may sometimes grow weary.'

Dione felt unexpected tears prick her eyes. No one had ever before appraised her situation so accurately, or commented upon it with such sympathy and understanding, and though she had sometimes thought dimly that it would be wonderful to have her responsibilities lifted from her by strong and capable hands, she had never felt, as she did now, that not only was this the one person with whom she could share that beloved burden, but that he was ready and willing to assume it. Considerably shaken by what must be, after all a mere delusion, she said unsteadily:

'You are right, of course. Ever since Papa died I have had to be, as it were, the man of the family.'

'I would not put it quite like that.' He sounded amused again, but the underlying warmth was still in his voice. 'However, to return to your immediate problem, what does Birkett intend to do now?'

'I was too angry to inquire, but I imagine he will write

to Eustace, who is shortly expected in town, and Eustace, no doubt, will do his utmost to persuade us to go back to London. At least he cannot compel us to give up Garth House.' A sudden doubt shook her, and she lifted an anxious face towards him, 'Can he?'

'Most unlikely, I should think, unless—is he Theodore's guardian?'

'Good gracious, no!' Dione rejected the suggestion with every appearance of disgust. 'When we were little, Papa's affairs were in the hands of an old shipmate of his, a captain under whom he had once served, but he died last year and no one was ever appointed to take his place. It did not seem necessary. I am of age, and perfectly capable of dealing with any problem which may arise.'

'Even a lawyer who refuses to discuss business with a female?' he suggested wickedly.

She laughed. 'Oh, I shall come about, sir, never doubt it! At last *Eustace* knows that I am not completely hen-witted, and though I dare say there will be a great deal of argument, I have only to stand firm, and persuade Mama to do likewise.'

His brows lifted. 'With the utmost respect to your mother, Miss Mallory, do you think you will be able to do that?'

'Oh, yes! You see, there is no doubt at all that already Theo is far better here than ever he was in London, and though Mama is in general very persuadable, she can be astonishingly firm where his wellbeing is concerned. We shall stay at Garth House.'

'And has Molly Ibstone refrained from playing ghost again?'

Dione hesitated. 'No,' she admitted at length, 'we have heard her more than once during the night. Or rather, Mama and Theo have heard her, for they are both very light sleepers. I must confess that her antics have not disturbed *me*.'

'No,' he murmured, 'I do not imagine that they would.' He parried with a smile the indignant glance she directed towards him, adding placatingly: 'You have already informed me, ma'am, that you have no belief in apparitions. I am astonished, though, that Theodore has not felt himself impelled to investigate these ghostly sounds.'

She chuckled. 'I dare say he would have done, sir, except that he knows very well that it is only Molly, and he *much* prefers to believe in a ghost.'

'You have not taxed the girl with it, or tried to catch her in the act?'

'No. Mama is still of the opinion that I should do so, but only consider the consequences. If I caught Molly playing ghost I could not punish her, except by turning her off, and I could scarcely do that, and expect her parents to continue in our service. Where, pray, could I find anyone to take their place, in an establishment such as Garth House? It is far better to feign ignorance, for she will tire of these tricks when she finds they are having no effect.' She paused, for they had reached a stretch of wall in a better state of preservation than the rest, with a narrow flight of steep steps winding upwards at one end. 'Is this where we must go to admire the view you spoke of?'

'It is, unless you have any objection to climbing these steps?'

'None, sir. I am not so poor-spirited.'

She withdrew her hand from his arm, lifted the hem of her skirt, and went nimbly in front of him up the flight. At the top, a level walk stretched the length of the wall, and afforded an undeniably magnificent view across miles of rolling countryside. Dione gave an exclamation of pleasure.

'Oh, you are right! It is truly breath-taking!'

They lingered there for some ten minutes, while he pointed out various landmarks in the prospect before them. Afterwards, as they descended from the battlements, Greydon taking Dione's hand to assist her down the steps, she halted on the lowest stair to say quietly:

'Thank you, Sir Greydon.'

He smiled. 'For showing you the view from the castle?'

'For everything. For driving me to town; for bearing with my ill humour and persuading me into a better one.'

She hesitated, and then added rather shyly: 'For understanding.'

He did not immediately reply. Standing as she was on the lowest step, her face was level with his so that they looked straight into each other's eyes. Dione became aware of an unfamiliar emotion, pleasurable and yet alarming. The hand he was holding trembled in his, and with the other she made a little, pleading gesture, entreating she knew not what. For an instant his grip tightened, but immediately relaxed again; he lifted her hand briefly to his lips, and then tucked it once more in his arm.

'Yes,' he said reassuringly, 'I understand. Come, I will take you home.'

Part 4

'Dee!' Theodore burst indignantly into the parlour, where his eldest sister was struggling, with indifferent success, to make sense of Mrs Ibstone's exceedingly haphazard household accounts. 'Did *you* tell Ibstone I was not to be allowed to go into the stables?'

'No,' she replied dampingly, 'and pray do me the kindness, Theo, of endeavouring to enter a room in a gentlemanly manner, and not as though you were a charge of cavalry.'

'I'm sorry, but, Dee, the stable door can't be opened. There is a big padlock on it.'

'There was a padlock on it when we arrived here.'

'Yes, I know, but I thought Ibstone would undo it when I told him I wanted to go in there.'

Dione laid down her pen and regarded him in bewilderment. 'Why in the world should you wish to do such a thing? There are no horses there.'

'I know. Ibstone keeps his old horse in one of the other buildings. I just wanted to see the stables. I may have a horse of my own one day.'

'By that time, my dear, if it ever comes, the stables will probably have fallen down,' she retorted ruefully. 'That is why the door is locked. Ibstone says the roof is unsafe.'

'It doesn't *look* unsafe.'

'Very likely not, but I think we must allow Ibstone to know more about that than we do. The stables have not been used for many years, for all Cousin Jonathan's horses were sold long ago, and so I dare say nothing has been done to keep the building in repair.'

'Nothing much has been done to the house, either, has it?' he remarked with devastating candour. 'Molly says that when it rains hard the roof leaks like a sieve.'

'What an enchanting prospect!' Dione said wryly. 'Do go away, Theo! I am too busy to listen to your chatter. Have you done the lessons I set you?'

'Oh, yes! Hours ago.' Theodore spoke airily, but then, realizing that this was perhaps unwise, hastily amended the statement. 'I *have* finished them, anyway. I'm sorry I disturbed you. I'll go and wait for Jem.'

He beat a hurried retreat, and Dione took up her pen again, reflecting that the improvement in Theo's health since coming to Garth House was an argument in favour of remaining there which would be useful when Eustace descended upon them and tried to insist upon them returning to London. Any such insistence Dione was determined to resist, and if occasional doubts troubled her, or the suspicion that Garth House in winter would be a very different proposition from Garth House in summer, she had so far managed to stifle them.

Theodore's cheerful reference to the state of the roof had recalled those doubts forcibly to her mind. Broken windows and a leaking roof would have to be somehow set to rights before the bad weather set in, and though Dione had no idea of the cost of such an undertaking, she had an uneasy feeling that it would be formidable. She must remember to ask Sir Greydon's advice next time she saw him.

It occurred to her as she sat there, thoughtfully brushing the feather of her pen to and fro against her chin, that seeking advice from Greydon Varleigh had become a habit with her. Just as visiting Garth House had, apparently, become a habit with him, for there were not many days when he failed to call upon them. Since the time he had driven her to town a closer understanding had been established between them; they had, she thought, become friends, and the knowledge of that friendship was warm and reassuring at the back of her mind even when she was not actually thinking of him.

She wondered sometimes, with a sinking heart, how she would go on when he was no longer at Rushbourne, and this thought led inevitably to speculation as to why he was there now. Dione had lived long enough in London to know that at this time of year people of fashion congregated there for the Season, for a concentrated whirl of social activity which lasted for several months before they dispersed again to their country houses, or transferred the pursuit of pleasure to Brighton and its nearby resorts. There must be some compelling reason for a fashionable man like Sir Greydon to isolate himself in the country at such a time. She had felt more than once that he was deeply troubled about something, and had wondered with anxious sympathy what it might be, but apparently they had not yet achieved a degree of intimacy where he felt the need to confide in her, no matter how much he encouraged her to confide in him. Perhaps, she reflected with unaccountable despondency, it was presumptuous of her to imagine that he ever would.

The task she had set herself was still not completed at dinner time, and after the meal, in spite of her mother's protests, she returned to it.

'I must finish the accounts tonight, Mama,' she said when Mrs Mallory urged her to leave them until the following day. 'I am just beginning to make sense of them, but after a night's sleep I would be as much at a loss as I was this morning. Besides, you know how I hate the task. If I complete it tonight I can go to bed with a clear conscience.'

Mrs Mallory sighed, but wasted no more breath upon arguments which she knew would prove futile. At ten o'clock she and Cecilia went upstairs, and Dione worked steadily on until, shortly before midnight, Mrs Ibstone's straggling columns of figures, on assorted scraps of paper which had been hopelessly muddled with bills and even one or two recipes, had been reduced to order and set out neatly on fresh pages in Dione's firm, capable writing. The tale they told was not encouraging, but she felt too tired to worry over it that night. Yawning, she lit her bedroom candle, extinguished the others and went slowly up the stairs, her feet in their light sandals making no sound on the ancient, solid oak boards.

Her eyes, strained by the long hours of poring over figures, were already heavy with sleep as she pushed open the door of the Great Bedchamber, and for a bemused moment she could not believe what they were telling her. Moonlight streamed through the window in the opposite wall, painting diamond-shaped patterns on the floor and mistily outlining the figure of a man which stood between the fireplace and the foot of the bed. Dione had a fleeting impression of a stooping, white-haired figure leaning on a stick, and then there was a whirl of movement, she gave a startled cry as the candle was dashed from her hand to extinguish itself on the floor, and something brushed past her and out of the door. She made an instinctive grab at it, set her foot on the fallen candle and fell heavily. Her head struck something with stunning force and everything dissolved into darkness.

She could have been unconscious for only a minute or two when her senses painfully returned, for Theodore was on his knees beside her, insistently calling her name, but though other agitated voices could be heard, no one else had yet arrived upon the scene. Apart from her brother and herself, the Great Bedchamber was empty.

'What is it? What has happened?' Mrs Mallory came hurrying in, still fastening her dressing-gown. A smothered shriek left her lips. 'Dee! Oh, merciful heaven!'

Cecilia and Edwina were close behind her, pale and frightened, anxious questions on their lips. Dione tried to answer, but had difficulty in marshalling her thoughts, and it was Theodore who offered a partial explanation.

'I heard a bump and a shout. It woke me up, and when I came to see what it was, I found Dee lying on the floor.'

'Oh, my poor girl!' Mrs Mallory dropped to her knees beside her daughter. 'Are you ill? What has happened to you?'

Edwina, practical still in spite of her fright, hurried into Theodore's room and fetched the lamp which Dione still kept burning there. As light brightened in the Great Bedchamber, Dione lifted a shaking hand to shield her eyes and said thickly:

'I tripped and fell. Pray help me up, Mama.'

Between them, Mrs Mallory and Cecilia got her to her feet and then on to the bed, where she sank weakly back against the pillows. She felt sick and giddy and her head was beginning to throb; more than anything she wanted to be left alone, to think, to try to remember, but first there was the family to be reassured.

'I tripped as I came into the room,' she repeated. 'I dropped my candle, and hit my head on something as I fell. It stunned me for a moment, that is all.'

Footsteps sounded in the corridor, a knock fell upon the half-open door, and Ibstone's voice was heard inquiring what was the matter.

'Miss Mallory has had a fall,' Mrs Mallory replied. 'Wait there, if you please. It may be necessary for you to fetch the doctor.' A vehement disclaimer from her eldest daughter interrupted her, and she added urgently: 'Dee, are you sure? A fall can be very dangerous.'

'Quite sure, Mama!' Dione forced herself to sit up, gritting her teeth against the way the room spun round her. 'Send Ibstone away. I would not dream of having Dr Bamfield called out at this hour for anything so trivial.'

Mrs Mallory seemed unconvinced, so Dione raised her own voice, bidding the manservant go back to bed, and after a moment's hesitation they heard him shuffle away. Dione looked at her mother.

'Truly, Mama, there is no need for a fuss. I feel a trifle bruised and shaken, and my head aches, but all I need is a good night's sleep.' She became aware of her brother, peering anxiously at her round the bed-curtain, and summoned up a smile. 'Go back to bed, Theo love. I'm sorry if I gave you a fright.'

'Yes, you did,' he replied with a hint of reproach. 'I thought you were dead.' He seized the hand nearest him in both his own, squeezing it hard. 'I'm glad you're not, Dee!'

Apparently ashamed of this unmanly betrayal of emotion, he then scurried off to his own room. Edwina, who had picked up and lighted Dione's candle, followed with the lamp.

'Very well, Dee,' Mrs Mallory said with a sigh. 'I know it is not the least use trying to persuade you, but I insist that you swallow a few drops of laudanum, to calm your nerves and make you sleep. I will go and fetch it, while Cecy helps you to bed.'

It seemed simpler to acquiesce, and Dione was in fact quite glad of her sister's aid as she undressed. She still felt dizzy, and a large, tender bump was beginning to form on the back of her head, so that even Cecilia's gentle fingers, unpinning the heavy coil of hair which had probably saved her from more serious injury, made her wince. She swallowed the laudanum without protest, submitted to having her forehead bathed with lavender-water, but heaved a sigh of relief when at last her mother and sister withdrew, leaving her to welcome darkness and silence.

Had she really seen that stooping, white-haired figure, or had it been a figment of her imagination, a kind of waking dream? And if she had seen it, who or what was it? Why was it there, and where had it gone? Had she dropped the candle, or had it been dashed from her hand? The questions seemed endless—and unanswerable.

* * *

Sir Greydon, about to drive his curricle through the overgrown gateway of Garth House, was obliged to rein in his team to allow another vehicle to emerge. This was Dr Bamfield's gig, and after exchanging greetings with its occupant, Greydon said with a frown:

'What brings you here, Bamfield? Has young Theodore been up to his tricks again?'

'No, not the boy. It is Miss Mallory who—!'

'Miss Mallory?' The question was rapped out in a tone which made the doctor blink. 'What has happened to her? Is she seriously ill?'

'No, no!' Dr Bamfield was reassuring, but looked very hard at Sir Greydon as he spoke. 'The young lady had a fall last night and struck her head, but fortunately sustained no more serious injury than a few bruises. Mrs Mallory sent for me this morning without her daughter's knowledge—and without, I may add, any real need, but she is inclined to be over anxious.'

'You are certain there is no cause for anxiety?'

'None whatsoever. Miss Mallory assures me—and I am prepared to believe her—that she is very rarely ill, and that a great deal of fuss had been made over very little. In fact, it was only with the greatest difficulty that I dissuaded her from undertaking whatever household business she had in mind for today.' He hesitated, cast another searching glance at the younger man from beneath bushy grey eyebrows, and then added bluntly: 'However, I am of the opinion, Sir Greydon, that Miss Mallory is troubled, though for what reason I do not know. She did not see fit to confide in *me*.'

Their eyes met; a look of understanding passed between them; Sir Greydon nodded.

'I am obliged to you, Bamfield. I will go and pay my respects to the ladies.'

With a brief word of farewell he drove behind the doctor's gig and disappeared into the green tunnel of the drive, leaving Dr Bamfield to go on his way in a very thoughtful frame of mind.

The front door of Garth House stood open to the warm summer day, and Cecilia, who chanced to be in the hall, greeted Sir Greydon with a shy smile, and the information that Mama and Dione were in the parlour. She led the way across the hall and opened the door, saying in her soft voice:

'Sir Greydon is here, Mama.'

Mrs Mallory exclaimed and rose to her feet, setting aside her seemingly interminable sewing, and gesturing to Dione, who was sitting in a big armchair by the window, to remain where she was. Sir Greydon shook hands with the elder lady and then turned to the younger, saying in a rallying tone but with a searching look:

'What is this I hear, Miss Mallory? I met Bamfield at the gate, and he told me that you have suffered an accident.'

'Oh, the stupidest thing!' she replied lightly, shaking hands with him. 'I was careless enough to trip as I went into my bedroom last night. I am ashamed to say that I created such a commotion that the whole household was awakened—for I had sat up late working on my accounts, and everyone else was in bed and asleep.'

'What a grossly unfair reward for diligence,' he said with a smile, thinking as he spoke that Bamfield was right. There was some trouble lurking in her eyes, though, as he had observed with satisfaction, this had been replaced for a moment by a look of relief when Cecilia announced his arrival. 'Bamfield spoke of a blow on the head. Are you sure you are well enough to be downstairs today?'

'Precisely what I said to her, Sir Greydon,' Mrs Mallory interjected triumphantly. 'Such an accident is bound to be a severe shock to the nerves, and she would be far better down upon her bed, in a darkened room.'

'I can imagine nothing, Mama, which would more certainly provoke a fit of the dismals,' Dione retorted, laughing. She looked up at Sir Greydon, this time with an unmistakable entreaty in her eyes. 'In fact, I was just thinking that what I would really like to do is walk in the garden, for I am sure I would feel a great deal better out of doors.'

He smiled understandingly down at her. 'An excellent notion! May I offer you the support of my arm, Miss Mallory?'

It was not to be supposed that this would meet with the approval of Mrs Mallory, who protested that Dione ought not to go out in the heat of the sun; that if she did, she must certainly put on a hat; then, when Dione protested that the thought of placing anything at all upon her head was unbearable, that she must carry her parasol, and sent Cecilia hurrying to fetch it. Dione bore this with commendable patience, assured her anxious parent that if she felt in the least faint she would return immediately to the house, and was at last allowed to go with Sir Greydon out of the parlour and through the hall.

'Thank you,' she said as they stepped out into the sunshine. 'I knew I could depend upon you to see that I need to speak privately with you, but I am sorry that Mama fusses so.'

'Her concern is very natural,' he replied. 'My only fear was that she might consider it necessary to send one of your sisters with us as chaperone.'

Dione chuckled. 'My dear sir, I am past the age of needing a chaperone.'

'My dear girl,' he retorted calmly, 'that is nonsense, and you know it.' He watched, with tender amusement, the colour rise suddenly to her pale cheeks, but kindly refrained from pursuing the subject. 'Where do you wish to walk?'

'Let us go into the rose-garden.' Dione had control over her voice if not her complexion. 'It is very pleasant there, though shockingly overgrown, of course.'

The rose-garden, surrounded by old stone walls, was sweet with perfume and loud with the humming of bees. The roses, unpruned for years, rioted everywhere in a triumphant medley of colour, and at the far end, where a great bush of them had climbed and spread to form a sort of bower, a curved stone seat was built into the wall. To this they made their way, but when they had sat there for a minute or two in silence, Greydon prompted gently:

'What did you wish to discuss with me?'

'I scarcely know how to begin.' Dione, who had furled her parasol when they entered the shadow of the rose-bower, prodded with the end of it at the moss growing between the flagstones at their feet. 'You will think me deranged, or, at the very least, one of those tiresome females for ever imagining all sorts of absurdities.'

'I can think of no circumstances which would cause me to do either,' he replied with a smile. 'Something happened last night, did it not? Something which you hesitate to confide to your family?'

'Yes,' she admitted. 'At least, I *think* it did. I cannot be sure, and that is what is worrying me more than anything else.'

Haltingly she described what had happened, watching him anxiously as she spoke. When she had finished, and he did not immediately reply, she added despondently:

'You do not believe me. I do not wonder at it.'

'My dear, of course I believe you.' He laid his hand briefly over hers as it rested on the handle of the parasol, and pressed it reassuringly. 'What we have to determine is whether there was, in fact, some intruder in your room, or whether fatigue merely caused you to imagine that you saw someone.'

'It could have been imagination,' she admitted. 'I was exceedingly tired. In fact, I could scarcely keep my eyes open as I went upstairs—you know how it is when one is almost asleep on one's feet. Yet I have a distinct impression that someone went past me out of the room.'

'Let us assume that you are right. We may rule out, I think, the possibility of an intruder, and that leaves only Ibstone. What, then, was he doing in your room?'

'Trying to frighten me by pretending to be Cousin Jonathan's ghost,' she replied promptly. 'Then, when I neither squealed nor fainted, he knocked the candle from my hand and made his escape.'

'Which brings us to the next question. *Why* try to frighten you?'

'I have been thinking a great deal about that,' she said confidentially, 'and I believe it may be because of that letter from Mr Birkett. Ibstone must know very well that if Garth House were sold, or hired out to a tenant, he and his family would have to leave, but if a rumour were put about that it is haunted—' she saw that he was looking sceptical, and added apologetically: 'It sounds absurd, I know, but can *you* think of a more plausible explanation?'

'To be honest with you, ma'am, I cannot,' he admitted ruefully, 'though if what you suppose is correct, I find it a trifle puzzling that he should seek to impose upon *you*.' He encountered a suspicious glance, and laughed. 'Do not look daggers at me! I meant merely that he must by now be sufficiently well acquainted with your family to realize that it would be far easier to alarm Mrs Mallory or Miss Cecilia. Unless, of course, it was Theodore whom he intended to frighten, and you arrived in time to prevent him.'

Dione laughed. 'No, no, Sir Greydon! You are quite out there, for nothing would please Theo more than to be convinced that Cousin Jonathan's ghost walks Garth House. He could then boast of it to Jem Durridge—!'

She broke off, and they looked at each other in silence as the same thought occurred to them both. Sir Greydon said softly:

'And young Durridge would tell the other boys in the village, and so the tale would be spread. Yes, if one accepts that Ibstone is fool enough to suppose that such a scheme would work, he could find no better way of spreading the rumour.'

'Well, that makes everything very simple,' Dione said with relief. 'All I need to do is to make it plain to the Ibstones that we have no intention of selling or leasing Garth House.'

He looked quizzically at her. 'In spite of what Birkett and your cousin say?'

'In spite of what *anyone* may say,' she retorted with a touch of defiance, resolutely ignoring the spectres of leaking roof and broken windows which forced themselves into her mind. 'This is the first time in our lives that we have lived in a house of our own, and nothing is going to persuade me to leave it.'

'Nothing, Miss Mallory?' Recklessly, Greydon decided to put his fortunes to the test. 'It is my hope—!'

'Dee!' Theodore's clear treble rang out, not far away and coming closer. 'Dee, where are you? Dee!'

'Here, Theo! In the rose-garden,' she replied, while Sir

Greydon with difficulty suppressed an exclamation of annoyance. 'What do you want?'

Her brother appeared under the stone archway which formed the entrance to the garden, then came down the steps and along the path towards them. He had all the appearance of a bearer of ill tidings.

'I've been looking everywhere for you,' he announced aggrievedly. 'Mama sent me to find you. Dee, the horridest thing has happened! Cousin Eustace has just arrived.'

* * *

No interruption, in Sir Greydon's opinion, had ever been more inopportune, yet his vexation was as much on Dione's behalf as his own. She was staring at Theodore in blank dismay.

'Eustace? Oh, not today, of all days! Theo, you are funning, are you not?'

'No, of course not! Cousin Eustace is nothing to joke about,' her brother retorted indignantly. 'He drove up in a post-chaise just after you and Sir Greydon came into the garden.' He fixed an anxious gaze upon her. 'Dee, he cannot make us go back to London, can he?'

'No, love, of course not! Where we live is no business of Eustace's. Go back now, and tell Mama that I will come directly.' She watched him trudge away, shoulders hunched, and then added with an attempt at lightness: 'How like Eustace, to arrive when I feel least able to deal with him! I must go in. Poor Mama will not know what to say.'

Resignedly Greydon got up and offered his arm. It seemed to him that she leaned upon it more wearily than before as they went towards the house, and he mentally consigned Eustace Winton to perdition.

'I do not believe, ma'am,' he ventured to say, 'that you are equal today to an argument with your cousin. Can you not go up to your room unobserved, and send word that you are not well enough to see him until tomorrow?'

'What, when he must know very well that I have been

in the garden with you?' she protested. 'For shame, Sir Greydon! Besides, if I did that, Mama would be obliged to invite him to stay the night, and I am hoping very much that he will take himself off after dinner. I dare say he will. He cares a great deal for his comfort, and Garth House is not at all what he has been used to.'

He could not help laughing a little at this, but amusement in no way lessened his concern for her. He found it very difficult to believe that Jack Ibstone had evolved an elaborate scheme to prevent Garth House passing into other hands, and thought it far more likely that Dione, being, on her own confession, asleep on her feet, had imagined or dreamed the mysterious presence in her room. This was disturbing, since it seemed to indicate that she had taken upon herself too heavy a burden of responsibility, and was even more worried than she cared to admit.

'Do not refine too much upon what happened last night,' he said as they went into the house. 'Even if what we were supposing is correct, Ibstone has probably been sufficiently frightened by the consequences of his trick to abandon the scheme. He is a surly, ne'er-do-well rogue, but I believe there is no real villainy in him.'

'Oh, I am not in the least afraid of Ibstone,' Dione assured him. She glanced towards the door of the parlour, and added in a lower voice, and with a little grimace: 'I am much more afraid that it will be almost impossible to convince Eustace that we have no intention of returning to London with him. He has the most antiquated notions, and firmly believes that all females are helpless, hen-witted creatures who must be tyrannized over by men for their own good.'

Greydon looked down at her, his dark eyes full of laughter. 'Then I can only say, Miss Mallory, that if long and close acquaintance with *you* has not shown him the error of that belief, he is past praying for.' He saw the answering laughter in her own eyes, and bent his head to murmur in her ear: 'I will come tomorrow to see how you go on, and if the tiresome fellow is still plaguing you, I promise to rid you of him. Very civilly, of course!'

It was perhaps unfortunate that Eustace Winton, instead of awaiting Dione in the parlour, should have taken it upon himself to inspect the rest of the ground-floor rooms, and at that moment emerged into the hall from a totally unexpected direction. He did not hear what Sir Greydon said, but he did hear Dione's little choke of laughter. He also saw, with outraged disapproval, that her hand was tucked confidingly into the arm of the tall, black-haired Corinthian who was whispering so intimately into her ear, and that, when she saw that they were no longer alone, she displayed none of the guilty embarrassment proper to a modest young woman discovered in a compromising situation. She merely withdrew the offending hand and extended it towards him, saying with cool civility and no pleasure whatsoever:

'Well, Eustace, this is indeed unexpected. I trust you left my aunt well?' She turned to her companion. 'Sir Greydon, may I present my cousin, Mr Winton? Sir Greydon Varleigh.'

The two men bowed, Sir Greydon with careless grace and Eustace stiffly, with disapproval in every line of his body. He saw, in the man before him, the personification of a world which a narrow, Nonconformist upbringing had taught him to abhor. He would have disliked and disapproved of Greydon Varleigh on sight whatever the circumstances of their meeting; the present situation merely exacerbated those feelings.

Sir Greydon had no difficulty in recognizing this antagonism. Mr Winton was something of a surprise to him, for Dione's reference to Eustace's regard for his own comfort had led him to expect a plump and probably foppish sybarite. Instead Winton was a man of spare build and somewhat dyspeptic appearance, and his clothes, though of excellent quality, had absolutely no pretension to fashion. He was, in fact, looking with undisguised contempt at the perfectly tailored riding-coat which fitted Varleigh's powerful frame like a second skin, at the intricately tied neckcloth, elegant buckskins and highly polished boots; he made no audible comment, but his expression implied a disparaging sniff.

Sir Greydon regarded him thoughtfully, with an infuriating glimmer of amusement lurking in his eyes, and then turned to Mrs Mallory, who had followed Eustace into the hall and was now hovering around them like an anxious and agitated butterfly.

'This is a family reunion, ma'am, and I must not intrude upon it,' he said, with an irony which only Dione appreciated, 'and so I will bid you good-day.'

He then bestowed on Dione herself a look of comically mingled commiseration and dismay which was almost too much for her gravity, and took leave of her and of Mr Winton. When he had gone, and they had rejoined the younger members of the family in the parlour, Eustace said to Mrs Mallory with an air of grave displeasure:

'I am sorry, ma'am, to find you upon terms with Sir Greydon Varleigh, whom I can only describe as an idle and worthless member of a world with which you and I, happily, have nothing to do.'

'Oh dear!' Mrs Mallory stared at him in dismay. 'But he has been most kind to us, Eustace, indeed he has.'

'And you can scarcely condemn as idle and worthless a man who served under the Duke of Wellington in Spain and in Belgium,' Dione added in a tone of barely suppressed anger, red danger signals flying in her hitherto pale cheeks. 'He spent twelve years in the army, you know.'

'I am aware of it, cousin, and I had no intention of decrying his *military* career,' Eustace replied stiffly. 'More recently, however, he has established himself as a leader of the Corinthians, a set of persons whose extravagant way of life cannot fail to disgust anyone not of an incurably frivolous turn of mind.'

'Sir Greydon's a great gun!' Theodore indignantly entered the fray in defence of his hero. '*He's* not for ever prosing on and on about duty and application and high principles. He drives prime cattle, too!'

'That, of course, is a recommendation of the highest order!' Eustace said acidly. 'Allow me to tell you, Theodore, that I perceive a sad deterioration in your manners in the short time since you left my house—an indication, if any were needed, of the justice of my observation.' He turned again to Mrs Mallory. 'Have the children no lessons they should be minding, ma'am? We have important matters to discuss.'

'Edwina,' Dione said hastily, before her youngest sister could voice the indignation she undoubtedly felt at being dismissed as a mere child, 'I have not yet felt equal to hearing the passages I set Theo to learn yesterday. Will you do it for me? You may take the books into the garden.'

'Of course, Dee. I will do anything I can to help *you*,' Edwina replied with dignity. 'Come along, Theo!'

They went out; Eustace turned an astonished and deeply disapproving look upon Dione.

'Into the *garden*?' he said, as though she had suggested instead the tap-room of the village inn. 'What, may I ask, is the matter with the schoolroom?'

'Nothing, except that, as yet, we have had no opportunity of establishing one,' Dione replied crisply. 'In fact, we have barely had time to settle into our new home, and you must forgive me for saying, Eustace, that it would have shown greater regard for our convenience if you had given us warning of your arrival. We are not really equipped to entertain guests.'

'Except, of course, for Sir Greydon Varleigh!' Eustace snapped. He then paused, compressed his lips, and drew a deep breath as though to control his temper before continuing in a more moderate tone: 'Cousin Dione, I did not come here to quarrel with you. I was appalled when I returned to London to find that you had embarked upon this ill-advised escapade, in spite of being very well acquainted with my views on the subject. It was not well done of you.'

'And was it well done of *you*, Eustace, to write to Mr Birkett instructing him to find a buyer or a tenant for Garth House, when you were very well acquainted with *my* views?'

'My only desire,' he retorted loftily (and with very little regard for the truth), 'was to relieve Aunt Mallory of the responsibility which had been thrust upon her. For Theodore's sake the inheritance was to be welcomed, but the administration of an estate, however modest, is not a matter with which a woman is capable of dealing.'

'Tell me, Eustace, have you yet made the acquaintance of Mr Birkett?' Dione asked with deceptive mildness. 'You and he should deal extremely together, for you both hold the same low opinion of female intelligence.'

'If you mean, cousin, that we both feel there is a certain impropriety in a woman endeavouring to deal with matters of business, you are right, but I have never held a low opinion of *your* intelligence. Your greatest fault lies in being headstrong, and in refusing to be guided by the advice of those wiser than yourself.'

'You are mistaken, Eustace. I am always prepared to listen to advice. What I will not submit to is tyranny.'

'Is it tyranny to be concerned for your welfare? For the welfare of all of you?' he demanded indignantly. 'To discover that you had left my house, had embarked upon a long journey—by stage-coach!— without a male escort, bound for a virtually unknown destination, filled me with the gravest misgivings. Even though you, ma'am,' turning to Mrs Mallory, 'had written to inform my stepmother of your safe arrival, I could not be easy without coming to see for myself how you went on. What I have found here shows me how right I was to be apprehensive.'

'And I am sure, Eustace, that we are all truly grateful for your concern,' Mrs Mallory assured him. 'It is very good of you to put yourself to so much trouble, but you must not be uneasy on our account. We are contriving very well, even though the house is not in as good repair as we might wish.'

'Not in as good repair?' he repeated. 'My dear aunt, it is little better than a ruin! You cannot seriously propose to remain here?'

'I could not seriously consider returning to London,' she replied. 'You can see for yourself how greatly Theo has benefited even in this short while, and *his* health, you know, must always be my first consideration.'

'He may benefit now, ma'am—and I will concede that he looks stouter than when I last saw him—but it will be a very different matter in winter. Even if the structure of this house is sound, which I doubt, it will be damp and draughty and almost impossible to keep warm. What will Theodore's health be like then?'

'No worse, and probably a great deal better, than in the London fogs,' Dione retorted. 'You know Dr Smithson told Mama that he would not answer for the consequences if Theo had to spend another winter in town.'

'So I recollect, and I recollect also that I offered to send Aunt Mallory, with Theodore and Edwina, to Bath for the duration of the bad weather. Naturally, that offer is still open, provided you abandon your foolish notion of living here, and return with me to London.'

'I am sure it is very generous of you, Eustace,' Mrs Mallory said earnestly, 'and we are very grateful, are we not, Dee? But we discussed this matter very thoroughly when we first arrived, and quite made up our minds that we are going to stay here.'

To this determination she clung, with a tenacity which startled even Dione, and no argument that Eustace could advance—and he advanced many—could persuade her to change her mind. As always when his will was crossed, he began to lose his temper, and made several very cutting remarks on the subject of folly and ingratitude and conceit (in supposing that they could contrive without his help and guidance) which reduced Cecilia to tears and prompted Mrs Mallory to remark that she must go and consult Mrs Ibstone about dinner. She then got up and drifted out of the room, a method of avoiding argument which she had perfected during the five years she had lived in the Winton household.

Dione looked at Cecilia, who was silently dabbing at her eyes with a damp handkerchief, and said with exasperated affection: 'For pity's sake, Cecy, there is no need to behave like a watering-pot! Eustace was not carping at you, were you, Eustace?'

'I trust,' he said coldly, 'that I am not carping, as you put it, at anyone. I have merely endeavoured to bring you, and Aunt Mallory, to your senses, but it is obvious that wiser counsels will not prevail. I can see that only bitter experience will demonstrate to you the depths of your folly, and so I am prepared to bide my time until life here becomes insupportable. Then, perhaps, you will be ready to admit that I am right.'

'Perhaps,' Dione agreed cordially. 'I should not depend upon it, though, Eustace, if I were you.'

He looked affronted, but instead of answering her, addressed his next words to her sister.

'Cecilia, would you be good enough to leave us alone? There is a matter upon which I wish to speak privately to Dione.'

It occurred to both girls that he might be intending to repeat his proposal of marriage, and Cecilia hesitated, looking doubtful, until a slight nod from Dione sent her thankfully from the room. Dione herself, facing Eustace with an air of polite attention, was hoping that this time she would be able to convince him that her refusal was final. Nothing, she realized now, could ever persuade her to marry him. It must be because she had not seen him for a while that she felt she was looking at him with fresh eyes, and it seemed incredible that she had ever considered, even for the family's sake, that she could bear to become his wife.

With her mind thus prepared to receive, and refuse, a proposal of marriage, Eustace's first words were as great a shock as a douche of cold water. Standing before the empty fireplace, hands clasped behind his back, he regarded her with an expression of portentous disapproval.

'I asked to speak privately with you, cousin, because I feel it my duty to warn you, to point out to you the perils attending the path you are so heedlessly treading.'

'To warn me?' she repeated blankly. 'Against what, for heaven's sake?'

'Say rather "against whom",' he replied sternly. 'Against Sir Greydon Varleigh, of course.'

'Against Sir Greydon?' She was furious with herself for repeating his words, parrot-fashion, but was so astonished that she could think of nothing else to say. 'What nonsense is this?'

'That you regard it as nonsense, cousin, indicates the

pass to which matters have already come. I am amazed at you, Dione! Amazed and shocked! When I learned from Birkett that you were escorted to his place of business by Varleigh, I could scarcely believe it.'

'Why not, pray? I was unable to hire a carriage, and Sir Greydon was obliging enough to drive me. Where is the harm in that?'

'You need to ask? You drive about the countryside, alone with this man, and you ask where is the harm?'

'Oh, don't be absurd!' she said angrily. 'In the first place, we were not alone. Sir Greydon's groom accompanied us. In the second, it is quite the thing for a gentleman to drive a lady. I have seen it a score of times in London.'

'People of fashion!' With the utmost contempt, Eustace dismissed the Polite World from his consideration. 'I should be sorry to see you seeking to imitate *their* conduct. Who, may I ask, presented Varleigh to you in the first place?'

This was less easy to answer. Dione knew that frankness would lead only to further argument, for which she felt disinclined. Her head was beginning to ache again, and her mother's recommendation that she should lie down in a darkened room seemed far more attractive than it had done earlier. She sought refuge in prevarication.

'You must remember, Eustace, that living in a village is very different from living in London. We have made the acquaintance of a number of people. The Vicar, Dr Bamfield and his family, Mrs Elverbury and her two daughters—'

'Yes, very likely,' he interrupted impatiently. 'All perfectly respectable people, no doubt, and I am not concerned with them. Varleigh is a different matter.'

'Are you suggesting, Eustace, that Sir Greydon is *not* respectable?'

'No,' Eustace retorted angrily, 'I am suggesting nothing. I am stating plainly that he is not a fit person for you to know.'

'How dare you!' Dione rose from her chair to confront him; her voice shook with anger. 'Who gave you the right to pass judgement upon my friends? *I* have never done so!'

'The mere fact that I am your only male relative gives me that right. No, wait!' As she made to speak again. 'Permit me to tell you a little about this friend you value so highly. He is the spoiled favourite of what is commonly referred to as "the *ton*". His life is spent in the heedless pursuit of pleasure, and his great wealth enables him to indulge himself in every extravagant whim. He gambles where the play is highest, squanders a fortune on his horses and his dress and—!'

Dione interrupted him ruthlessly. 'I had no notion, Eustace, that you were so closely acquainted with Sir Greydon! How foolish you must have thought me, when I presented you to him as though you had never met before.'

'This is no matter for levity, cousin! Naturally, when I learned of his acquaintance with you I took the trouble to inform myself fully of his character and his habits. What I discovered filled me with the gravest misgivings on your behalf.'

'I should be grateful, no doubt, that you put yourself to so much trouble, but I am the oddest creature! I have a positive aversion to anyone who pries into my concerns, or those of my friends. All that you say about Sir Greydon may be true—I neither know nor care! To me—to all of us—he has been unfailingly kind.'

Eustace studied her in silence, frowning heavily. He took a turn about the room and then returned to his former position by the fireplace, while she watched him impatiently.

'Dione,' he said gravely at length, 'you are not a schoolgirl. Surely you realize that Sir Greydon Varleigh is what is vulgarly known as a "brilliant catch"? If he chooses to marry, he may look for his bride among the highest in the land, young women of rank and fortune.'

She stared speechlessly at him for a moment, and then demanded in outraged tones: 'Eustace! Are you implying—do you *dare* to imply that I have been *setting my cap* at Sir Greydon?'

'What else am I to suppose,' he retorted angrily, 'when

I find you hanging upon his arm while he whispers in your ear in an intimate manner which even *I* would not venture to assume with you? I have never been more shocked in my life! I am aware that he is known, even among his own set, as a dangerous flirt, but I never imagined that you—!'

'Is he, indeed? No doubt that is another piece of information gleaned by your spying.'

'It is one which I hoped not to be obliged to impart, but I see I have no choice. You are deluding yourself, cousin! It is out of the question that Sir Greydon Varleigh will ever offer you marriage.'

'I did not suppose that he would! Such a thought never entered my mind!'

'The more shame to you, then, for permitting him the degree of familiarity which I witnessed between you! I think you must have taken leave of your senses! Even if you were unaware of *his* reputation, to have so little regard for your own—!'

'That is enough!' Dione spoke quietly, but in a tone which pierced even his armour of self-righteousness. 'I will listen to no more insults and innuendos. Pray go! I will make your excuses to Mama.'

He stared at her, his face white and spiteful. 'If I go, cousin, it will be for good. Do not imagine that you will be able to come to me for help when you find yourself at a standstill.'

'Nothing would ever induce me to do so!'

'We'll see that! I suppose you are depending upon your *friend* Varleigh to rescue you from the consequences of establishing yourself in this mouldering ruin of a house, but be warned, Dione! There are aspects of his life of which, to spare your blushes, I have not spoken, but you may find, when it comes to the point, that you are not prepared to pay the price he will demand of you.'

'Oh, let us not be mealy-mouthed!' By now Dione had lost her last precarious hold upon her temper. 'You mean, do you not, that you think Sir Greydon will invite me to become his mistress? Well, let me tell you, Eustace, that I would far sooner accept a *carte blanche* from him than a proposal of marriage from you! Now go! I wish never to see you again!'

'You will not, ma'am! You may be sure of that!' He strode furiously to the door and flung it open, then paused to look back at her, apparently at a loss for words. Then, ejaculating: 'Shameless, shameless!' he went out, and the door slammed behind him.

Dione sank down into her chair, pressing her hands to her scarlet cheeks. Eustace's parting words, she thought, were justified. It *was* a shameless thing to have said, even under the goad of extreme provocation. Young, unmarried women were supposed to know nothing of such matters, and if this supposed innocence was largely an illusion cherished by the opposite sex, it was an illusion which ought not to be openly shattered. She was honestly appalled by what she had said; even more appalling was the suspicion, no sooner recognized than thrust guiltily aside, that it might possibly be the truth.

* * *

Dione slept badly that night, a fact which she had no hesitation in ascribing to an unquiet conscience. Not that the rest of the family blamed her for quarrelling irretrievably with Eustace, Edwina and Theodore being openly jubilant, and Cecilia resigned. Mrs Mallory, to whom Dione admitted privately that her dismissal of Eustace might prove to have been improvident, said vaguely but with unusual optimism that she was sure it would all turn out for the best; she had no wish to return to London, and was thankful to be spared further argument. Dione was not to refine upon it any more.

This maternal advice Dione found herself unable to adopt. She had dismissed with no more than a moment's consideration Eustace's suspicion that Sir Greydon was bent upon seducing her. She fancied she knew him rather better than to believe that, and in any event (with a touch of wry humour), it was unlikely that with all the beautiful and accomplished women in London to choose from, he would waste a moment's amorous consideration upon her. He was a kind friend, but though she had no hesitation in turning to him for advice, she would not dream of asking for more material assistance.

Yet assistance she was more than likely to need. As she tossed restlessly in her huge, forbidding bed the thought of her many responsibilities crowded about her like mocking phantoms. The house, the 'mouldering ruin' as Eustace had contemptuously but with some justification described it, which threatened to make continuous and heavy demands upon a very slender purse, was the most immediately menacing, but close upon its heels came the question of Theodore's education. As soon as his health had sufficiently improved, he would need proper schooling, and where was the money for that to come from? Then there were Cecy and Edwina, who deserved some brighter prospect than being mere spinster daughters in an impoverished household; and Mama—how long would her delicate constitution support the rigours of life at Garth House once the summer was over?

With a little moan of despair Dione buried her face in her pillow. Her family might not blame her for quarrelling with Eustace, but by now she was bitterly blaming herself. Until today there had still been a refuge to which, even at the cost of some personal sacrifice, she could have returned the family if circumstances made it impossible to remain at Garth House, but now there was nowhere to turn. 'Burning her bridges' Greydon had called it when she described how she had parted from Aunt Winton; she had burned them now with a vengeance, and all because she had allowed Eustace to goad her into quite unpardonable behaviour.

It was scarcely surprising that morning found her as pale as before, the shadows about her eyes more pronounced. Mrs Mallory, much concerned, wanted to send again for the doctor, but Dione brushed the suggestion aside, declaring that she would be better directly. She made a pretence of eating breakfast, half-heartedly assayed several household tasks, and then, to escape her family's anxious concern, wandered out into the garden.

She could not, however, escape from her problems, and was walking dispiritedly beside the pool, through the long grass starred with daisies and buttercups which had once been a lawn, when Sir Greydon drove up in his curricle. As soon as he caught sight of her he pulled up, handed the reins to Stubbs, and alighted to come quickly towards her. As they shook hands he looked searchingly into her face, saying with swift concern:

'I had hoped to find you more recovered than this. What has happened? Is that tiresome fellow, Winton, still here?'

She smiled rather wanly. 'No, he did not stay very long. To tell truth, I rid myself of him, though not, I fear, very civilly. So *un*civilly, in fact, that he will never come here again.'

'And now you are blaming yourself for having done so,' he said shrewdly. 'What you need, Miss Mallory, is some diversion to give your thoughts a new direction. Will you let me take you for a drive?'

She hesitated, thinking of work undone, but the temptation was too strong to resist. If she could get away from Garth House for a little while, she thought, perhaps she would be able to view her problems in a new light, and find them not so troublesome after all.

'Thank you. I would enjoy that. Will you come in and talk to Mama while I get ready? I will not keep you waiting above ten minutes.'

Mrs Mallory, informed of the intended outing, gave it her unqualified approval, confiding to Sir Greydon, while her daughter was upstairs, that she did not care to see Dione looking so worn. It was not like her; she had inherited her Papa's excellent constitution, and even the unfortunate accident two nights before should not have pulled her down so.

'I fancy, ma'am, if you will forgive me for saying so,' he replied bluntly, 'that it was the visit you sustained yesterday from Mr Winton, more than her fall, which is at the root of Miss Mallory's indisposition.'

'Yes, indeed,' she agreed earnestly. 'What passed between them I do not know, but I do not scruple to tell you, Sir Greydon, that when he came to take leave of me, he informed me that we would never see him here again.' She sighed. 'His intentions are good, you understand, and his concern for us genuine, but to state that we could not possibly remain here, and to tell Dee that she is headstrong, and should be guided by the advice of those wiser than herself, was *not* the way to go about things.'

His lips twitched. 'Most decidedly not. I hesitate to inquire what reply Miss Mallory made to that.'

'She told him that she was always ready to listen to advice, but would never submit to tyranny.'

'Did she?' he said appreciatively. 'You know, ma'am, I cannot help feeling that their quarrel was inevitable, for it seems to me that Mr Winton has not the smallest notion how to remain on good terms with your daughter.'

'He never had,' she admitted, 'and it was most unfortunate that he should have chosen to visit us just when she is feeling out of sorts. In the ordinary way, such a disagreement with him would not have troubled her in the least.'

'Perhaps,' Greydon suggested, 'Miss Mallory is concerned on your behalf, ma'am. She may fear that a breach between her and Mr Winton may lead to one between you and your sister, and thus cause you distress.'

The widow looked much struck. 'That had not occurred to me! She has said nothing to indicate—! Sir Greydon, if she should hint such a thing to you, I beg that you will do your best to reassure her. I have a sincere regard for my sister, but her claim upon my affection lags far behind my daughter's.' She paused, eyeing him rather defiantly. 'Does that shock you, sir? Do you perhaps feel that I place too high a value upon Dione?'

He smiled and shook his head. 'My dear Mrs Mallory, to do that were impossible. She is beyond price.' Their eyes met for a moment, but before anything more could be said Dione herself came back into the room, with her hat on, and carrying a sunshade, and he added lightly: 'Miss Mallory, you must allow me to congratulate you. You are the first lady I have ever known to say ten minutes, and mean it.'

They took leave of Mrs Mallory, and went out. A few minutes later Cecilia came hurrying into the room, looking concerned.

'Mama, did you know that Dee has driven out with Sir Greydon?'

'Yes, my love. He was here for a few minutes, talking to me while she put on her hat.'

'But, Mama, what can Dee be thinking of? They have gone *alone*! Sir Greydon told his groom to wait here.'

Mrs Mallory received this shocking intelligence with admirable calm. Her head bent again over her sewing, but Cecilia saw with astonishment that a little, pleased smile was playing about her lips.

'Did he, my love?' she said placidly. 'Well, no doubt he had some good reason for doing so.'

* * *

'You do not object, I trust, to leaving Stubbs behind?' Greydon remarked as he guided his team cautiously along the drive. 'I recollect that you told me yesterday you consider yourself past the need for a chaperone.'

'Yes, and *I* recollect that you told me yesterday you consider yourself past the need for a chaperone.'

'Yes, and *I* recollect the answer you made,' she retorted. 'I do not object, of course. I have often thought it must be exceedingly uncomfortable for the poor man to be perched up behind us in that fashion, and quite unnecessary, after all.'

'Most people consider it necessary in order to observe the proprieties.'

'I wonder why?' she said reflectively. 'It is hard to imagine *what* impropriety could take place in an open carriage with the driver fully occupied in handling a team of spirited horses.' She cast him a somewhat uncertain glance, saw that he was laughing, and added contritely: 'I ought not to have said that. It betrayed a sad want of delicacy.'

'On the contrary, it is a delightfully practical point of view.'

'How comfortable it is to be able to say what one

thinks,' she remarked. 'Do petty shibboleths of that sort put *you* out of patience, too?'

'Frequently,' he admitted cheerfully. 'I think it must be because of the years I spent in the Peninsula, where life was a great deal more free and easy.'

'Tell me about it,' she said suddenly. 'The campaigns there, I mean. Some of Papa's friends were used to visit us from time to time, so I learned a little about the war at sea, but I have never met an army officer before.'

A little amused, but pleased by this evidence of interest, he did as she asked. He had had a distinguished career in a famous regiment, but he scarcely touched upon that, and as they drove along the road that led away from the village and climbed the hills behind Garth House, he instead talked entertainingly of the life in Spain and Portugal, the long summer campaigns and the boredom of winter quarters. She listened with complete absorption, asked an occasional question, and eventually said:

'Did you always wish to join the army? It seems to me that you enjoyed it very much.'

He laughed. 'Yes, I was army-mad from a very early age, and I did enjoy it. That is to say, life on active service suited me exactly, but I had no taste for peacetime soldiering.'

'Is that why you sold out?'

'That, and the fact that my grandfather had died while I was still in Spain, and it was time, so my grandmother informed me, that I came home to take up my responsibilities. She had been against my entering the army at all, since I am the only surviving male Varleigh, but fortunately for me my grandfather was not of the same opinion.'

They were driving now along the crest of the hills and Rushbourne Abbey was plainly in view in the valley below. The great house and its surrounding gardens; the tree-dotted expanse of parkland; the Home farm and all the other attendant buildings, looking, as Theodore had said, almost as large as a village. Dione studied it thoughtfully, and then glanced again at her companion.

'Yet one cannot but sympathize with her ladyship's feelings,' she remarked. 'How thankful she must be to have you safe home.'

'Yes, though she is moved at times—when she is particularly out of patience with me, you know—to inform me that since I seem bent upon breaking my neck in the hunting field, or at some other sporting pastime, I might as well have stayed in the army. My grandmother, Miss Mallory, is not given to displays of sentiment.'

Dione chuckled appreciatively. 'As I said, sir, one cannot but sympathize with her ladyship,' she observed demurely. She glanced sidelong at him, met his eyes, and chuckled again.

'Yes,' he said grimly, but with an answering tremor of laughter in his voice, 'you and she will deal extremely together, I have no doubt.'

'I am flattered that you think so, sir. I collect that her ladyship does not reside at the Abbey?'

'She is in London at present. Though she does not now go very much into society, she likes to be there for the Season. I expect her at Rushbourne later in the summer.'

He was silent for a moment, and Dione saw that he was frowning. Once again she had the impression that he was deeply troubled; she was conscious of a rush of sympathy and conern, and of an urgent wish that he would see fit to confide in her.

'When my grandmother does come,' he resumed after a moment, 'and there is a hostess at Rushbourne, I look forward to the pleasure of welcoming you there.'

Dione was startled, for even in the short while she had been in Brambledon, she had learned that invitations to the Abbey were not easily come by. Mrs Elverbury, condescending to chat to Mrs Mallory after church, had been at some pains to make that clear, and to indicate that though Sir Greydon might beguile the time by calling at Garth House, the Mallory family need not flatter themselves that they were therefore upon terms with the Varleighs.

'We should be honoured, Sir Greydon,' she replied, 'if Lady Varleigh is kind enough to invite us. I am told that the Abbey is a most interesting house.'

'It is an architectural hotch-potch,' he replied cheerfully, 'but we are sincerely attached to it, and Theodore, I feel certain, will be impressed to learn that we really do have a ghost. A white monk—the Abbey was a foundation of the Carmelite order—who may occasionally be observed walking where the cloisters once stood.'

'Impressive, indeed!' she observed politely. 'Have *you* ever encountered this interesting apparition, sir?'

'I have not had the privilege, Miss Mallory,' he confessed solemnly, 'though there are numerous apparently well-authenticated accounts of its appearance at intervals during the past two hundred and fifty years, and my Aunt Georgiana—Vivyan Calderwood's mother—will tell you that she once caught a glimpse of it when she was a girl. My aunt,' he added pensively, 'has always been a person of extreme sensibility.'

'Ah!' Dione said understandingly. 'Then I do not suppose that *I* would ever see your ghost, sir.'

He glanced at her with some amusement. 'You do not consider yourself a person of sensibility?'

She shook her head. 'Alas, no! Common sense is my forte, and I am sure no ghost would ever manifest itself to anyone as prosaic and practical as I.' She laughed. 'That would sink me beyond reproach in Theo's eyes, would it not? How fortunate that we shall have no opportunity to put it to the test.'

'Why not?' he asked calmly. 'I hope that we may have every opportunity.'

She looked astonished, but then laughed. 'Oh, come, Sir Greydon! Do not try to convince me that your white monk is in the habit of appearing to morning-callers. Surely, in the best tradition of ghost stories, he walks only at midnight, or appears to no one but members of the family?'

'Exactly so. Will you marry me, Dione?'

For a few stunned seconds she thought she must be dreaming, that the imagination she had just denied possessing was playing tricks on her. She turned a startled, questioning glance towards him, realized that he had indeed uttered those incredible words, and said in a shaken voice:

'You cannot be serious! Nothing could be more unsuitable.'

'No?' His tone was quizzical. 'From your point of view, ma'am, or from mine?'

'Why—why, from yours, of course!'

'Could you not perhaps allow *me* to be the judge of that? *I* can think of nothing more desirable.'

She was silent, turning her head to look out over the sunlit prospect below them. After a little he said gently:

'Are you thinking of your family? Set your mind at rest. It will be my pleasure as well as my duty to look after them.'

She felt tears fill her eyes, and blinked them angrily away. Eustace's taunts of the day before came into her mind, and then the memory of the night's black despair. She had been crushed beneath the weight of worry and self-reproach, not knowing which way to turn; now, suddenly, when courage and hope had sunk to their lowest ebb, the load was to be lifted from her shoulders for ever. She had but to say one word, and all the doubts and fears which had made the night hideous would be dispersed like the darkness itself. It was so simple, and yet...

'It *would* be unsuitable,' she said in a low voice. 'Your family would be horrified. Your grandmother—!'

'My grandmother desires nothing so much as to see me married.'

'But not to me, to a nobody. I am not fitted to take *her* place at Rushbourne.'

'You would grace any house you chose to live in, and as for being a nobody, there has been a Mallory in Brambledon almost as long as there has been a Varleigh.'

'I must try to make you understand,' she said urgently, turning to him again. 'You cannot deny that our situations are so vastly different that to make me an offer at all you must feel an—an uncommon regard for me—!'

'Oh, let us not mince matters, my darling!' he

interrupted, laughing. 'I love you as I never thought I could love any woman, as a friend and companion as well as the most enchanting and adorable creature I have ever met.'

'Do not! Oh, pray do not!' Dione pressed her hands to her hot cheeks. 'I never dreamed—! I am not in the least like that. So ordinary, so—so *un*accomplished!'

'I cannot imagine,' he remarked, 'how you come to have such an astonishingly low opinion of yourself. Your family, quite rightly, value you beyond price. I am doing my best to convince you that you have become by far the most precious thing in the world to me.' He cast a quick glance at her, saw tears sparkling on her lashes, and, bringing the curricle to a halt beneath the spreading branches of a wayside oak, added in a quite different tone: 'My dearest, what have I said to make you cry?'

'I do not know!' Dione hunted in her reticule for a handkerchief and resolutely dried her eyes. 'I have the greatest contempt for females who weep for no reason at all.' She blew her nose in a determined manner, and put the handkerchief away. 'Let us try to be sensible, dear sir. You have made me a very flattering offer and I am truly honoured—'

'Do you know,' he broke in conversationally, 'this is the first time I have ever known you to be missish? It does not suit you, my love.'

'Pray listen to what I have to say,' Dione begged. She stared straight ahead, across the tossing heads and glossy coats of the four fretting, sidling black horses, trying to ignore the endearments he addressed to her, and the caressing tone of his voice. It would be all too easy to succumb, to accept his proposal and with it an end to the seemingly ceaseless worry and the struggle to make ends meet. So easy, and so unfair to him. 'No matter how you may deny it, such a marriage would be regarded by your family and friends as a shocking *mesalliance*, which indeed it would be. You say you—you care for me enough for that not to matter to you, but I—!'

'But you do not care for me in the same way,' he concluded in an expressionless voice as she hesitated. 'I understand.'

'But you don't!' she said desperately. 'I would like very much to marry you, but I cannot tell whether or not it is for the right reason. I am in such a fix, you see. There is the house, and Theo's education, and now that I have quarrelled past mending with the Wintons, I do not know which way to turn. You offer me so much! How could I be sure, if I accepted your proposal, that it was not just to find a way out of my difficulties?' She turned to look at him again, still with heightened colour, but meeting his eyes squarely as she added rather shyly: 'Oh, I know that we are friends, but that would not be enough, would it?'

'No,' he replied with equal honesty, 'it would not, but I do not despair of convincing you that you would like to marry me for the *right* reason. And the next time I propose to you,' he added forcefully as the carriage jerked to the restless movements of the horses, 'it will not be in a curricle, with a spirited team in hand.'

She smiled, but said rather wistfully: 'I think perhaps you ought not to propose again at all. I am really quite ineligible, you know.'

'Miss Mallory,' Greydon informed her, setting the horses in motion again, 'I shall propose to you at every possible opportunity until I persuade you to accept me. I do not, I warn you, readily accept defeat.'

She could think of nothing to say. It would not, she thought, be easy to resist him for very long, but she could not rid herself of the conviction that for his sake she ought to. Perhaps the wisest course, she reflected with a sudden sense of desolation, would be to take care that the opportunities he spoke of did not occur.

The road they followed had brought them to the crest of Garth Hill, along the road where they had met when she was searching for Theodore. Greydon spoke of that now, lightly, inquiring whether there had been any similar escapades, and whether the budding friendship between Theo and Jem Durridge had flourished. Dione, recognizing his intention of relieving any awkwardness between them, responded gratefully.

'Indeed it has. Of course, Jem has a good deal of work to do upon the farm, but most of his leisure is spent with Theo. You were quite right. It has done Theo a great deal of good, for this is the first time he has been upon terms of friendship with a boy of his own age.'

They continued to converse upon this and other safe topics while they descended the hill and turned along the road which led past Garth House to Brambledon and Rushbourne. Just short of the entrance to the drive, they rounded a bend to see a phaeton and pair coming towards them, and with an exclamation of astonishment Sir Greydon reined in his team.

'Vivyan!' he greeted the driver of the other carriage. 'What the deuce brings you here?'

Dione thought that there was something more than surprise in his voice; she detected an undertone of anxiety, while a quick glance at his profile informed her that the frown had returned. She transferred her gaze to Mr Calderwood, who had brought his phaeton to a halt abreast of the curricle, and read unmistakable relief in his face.

'This is a stroke of good luck, Grey, meeting you like this! I was on my way to Rushbourne to find you.' He lifted his hat to Dione. 'Servant, Miss Mallory.'

She bowed her acknowledgement. Greydon said impatiently:

'To find me? Why?'

'Came to warn you,' Vivyan replied. 'Grandmama's on her way! In fact, she should be arriving at Rushbourne within a couple of hours.'

* * *

'A couple of hours?' Greydon repeated incredulously. 'We have had no word! Nothing is prepared, her apartments are still closed—!'

'Wanted to surprise you!' Vivyan looked uncomfortable. 'I didn't find out about it myself until last night, for I've been out of town for a few days, but I met Mama at Lady Butterworth's ball, and was informed that Grandmama had set out that morning, and that you knew nothing about it. Well, I knew she would take two days for the journey and that she always stops for the night at the "Mitre", so I made my excuses, stayed only for my man to pack a few necessities, and came straight away. Luckily there was a full moon!'

'I'm obliged to you, Viv. Did you pass Grandmama on the road?'

Vivyan grinned. 'Lord, no! Of course, by the time I got to the "Mitre" this morning she had been gone for hours, but you know how the old lady travels. Her own carriage, outriders, a chaise for the servants and one for the baggage—a real state progress! All the gatekeepers know her, so when I found I was close on her heels I turned off the main road and came cross-country, hoping against hope that I'd find you at home.'

There was a brief pause. Sir Greydon was still frowning, Vivyan looking harassed, and Dione knew beyond all doubt that something was very wrong indeed. At length Greydon said abruptly:

'Do you know what prompted her to leave London so suddenly?'

'Yes,' Vivyan replied reluctantly, 'I do.' He hesitated, and then addressed the groom who was seated impassively beside him. 'Get down, Hicks, and walk on along the road. I'll take you up again directly.' He waited until the man had obeyed and was out of earshot, and then went on: 'Mama showed her a letter she had received from Mrs Elverbury. Silly thing to have done, for she might have known it would set the cat among the pigeons, which I'll lay odds was what the confounded woman was hoping for.'

'A letter from Mrs Elverbury?' Greydon's tone had sharpened. 'About what, pray?'

Vivyan looked acutely embarrassed. 'Oh, a lot of spiteful nonsense. You know what an old tabby she is! I told Mama she ought not to have regarded it, much less shown it to Grandmama, but by then, of course, the harm was done. Fact is, Grey, Miss Mallory's name was mentioned.' He saw the sudden leap of anger in his cousin's eyes, and nodded. 'Aye, just so! Mischief-making old gossip!' He turned to Dione, adding earnestly: 'Make you my apologies, ma'am. No wish to disturb you, but I thought you ought to know.'

'Yes. Thank you,' she replied in a stifled voice, not

looking at him. 'You are very kind.'

Greydon looked quickly at her averted face. She had flushed scarlet at Vivyan's disclosure, but was now very pale, and he could see that she was trembling, though whether with distress or anger he could not tell. Subduing his own anger, he turned again to his cousin.

'Will you drive on to Rushbourne, Viv, and warn them of our grandmother's impending arrival? I will follow you as soon as I have taken Miss Mallory home.'

Mr Calderwood nodded understandingly, bowed to Dione and set his horses in motion again. Sir Greydon, doing likewise, said quietly:

'It would be useless, I know, to advise you to disregard what has happened, but try not to let it distress you too much. I will not allow it to hurt you, you know.'

'How dare she!' Dione's voice was shaking with anger, 'How dare she try to stir up trouble between you and your grandmother! *I* am not important—I know she does not like me—but she ought to have some regard for Lady Varleigh's feelings. It is despicable, deliberately to set out to anger and distress an old lady!'

'Anger, most certainly,' he agreed, 'but my grandmother, I assure you, is more than a match for Mrs Elverbury, especially since she has known the lady since her nursery days. As to yourself, do I need to repeat that you are far more important to me than anything else?'

'Pray do not say that,' she said unsteadily. 'It would not do—you know it would not! You have known it all along, no matter how you may try to convince yourself otherwise.'

He turned his head to smile at her. 'And what makes you imagine that?'

'I have not imagined it. I have felt more than once that you are gravely troubled about something, but until today I never suspected what it was. Then, when Mr Calderwood told you that Lady Varleigh was on her way, you looked so very shocked and dismayed, and I *knew*.'

'I was shocked and dismayed, my love, for reasons which are in no way concerned with you.'

'Please,' she said with difficulty, 'you must not call me

that! I could not bear to be the cause of trouble between you and your family.'

They had reached the gateway of Garth House, and Greydon did not reply until he had guided his team through the narrow entrance and gone far enough along the drive for the road to be out of sight. Then he brought the curricle to a halt and turned to face her.

'Yes, I am troubled,' he said wryly, 'and exceedingly dismayed that my grandmother is about to arrive at Rushbourne, but that is because of something which happened before I had the inestimable good fortune to meet you. I can see, however, that the only way to convince you of that is to tell you the real cause of my uneasiness. No'—for she had started to protest—'bear with me for a few minutes, Dione. There must be no misunderstanding between you and me.'

Briefly he outlined the story of the Varleigh Medallion, its theft by Oliver Varleigh and Oliver's subsequent disappearance. She listened in shocked silence, and when he had done, laid her hand on his arm.

'I am so very sorry,' she said simply. 'Will you be able to keep it from her, do you think?'

'I do not know. It may be possible, for I doubt whether she has even seen the Medallion for a decade or more, but if she were to take a sudden fancy to have it fetched from the strong-room, to show to someone, perhaps, the truth would be bound to come out.'

'I suppose,' Dione suggested diffidently, 'that you could not have a replica made, so that Lady Varleigh need never know that your cousin stole anything but the money? I know it would not be quite honest, but for the sake of Lady Varleigh's peace of mind—!'

'The idea had occurred to me,' he admitted, 'but unfortunately no sufficiently detailed drawing of the Medallion exists.'

'You no longer have any hope of recovering it? Perhaps the Bow Street Runners—?'

'They have had little enough success up to now. In London they have discovered nothing at all, while the fellow who was sent here has so far been able to tell me only that Oliver was heavily in debt, which I already knew, and in the clutches of an unscrupulous money-lender, which I did not know but which surprises me not at all. I am expecting the man to report to me again tomorrow, but have very little hope that he will have anything of importance to tell me.'

'If he had,' Dione asked curiously, 'and if you found your cousin and recovered the Medallion, what would you do about Mr Varleigh himself?'

'Pay his debts and ship him out of the country,' Greydon replied promptly. 'I have no desire for revenge, only to be rid of him, and provided he never returned to England he would have nothing to fear from me.' He paused, quizzically regarding her. 'Well, ma'am, have I succeeded in convincing you that my dismay at Vivyan's news was not in any way upon your account?'

'Yes,' she admitted, 'but not that if Lady Varleigh knew you had proposed to me she would not dislike it excessively.'

'*When* she knows,' he corrected her gently, 'for I have every intention of telling her, I do not deny that she will be displeased at first, but when she knows *you*, my love, it will be a different matter. I was not jesting when I said that you and she will deal extremely together, so do not fear that when you marry me you will be joining a family hostile to you.' She made a little gesture of protest, but he only smiled and shook his head. 'You *are* going to marry me, you know.'

'If only I could be *sure* of what I feel!' she said breathlessly. 'You see, Eustace Winton wanted to marry me, too, and there was a time, just after we arrived at Garth House and found it so different from our expectations, when I almost decided to accept him. And I do not even *like* him.'

'I am not in the least surprised,' Greydon agreed comfortingly. 'I do not like him myself.'

'But do you not *see*? If I could think of marrying a man I do not like, just because he would provide for me and my family, how can I be certain, when I like *you* so much, that that is not the reason—!' She broke off, halfway between tears and laughter. 'And it is too bad of you to laugh at me, when I am so confused.'

'My poor darling!' Greydon transferred the reins to his whip hand, and possessed himself of one of hers. 'How can I help it, when you talk such nonsense? Never mind! I can see that I took you too much by surprise, so for the present I will ask only that you think about what I have said, though it is only fair to warn you that if I were not obliged to hasten back to Rushbourne—and if I could rid myself of these confounded horses—I would do my best to help you to arrive at a decision with no more delay.'

Part 5

A little less than the two hours predicted by Vivyan had passed when Lady Varleigh's luxurious travelling carriage drew up before the main door of Rushbourne Abbey, but her reception left nothing to be desired. Dobson, the butler, and his wife, who was the housekeeper, had risen nobly to the challenge presented by Mr Calderwood's announcement, and had urged their numerous underlings to such activity that her ladyship's apartments were ready to receive her, even to fresh flowers in the vases, while the chef was rapidly revising the planned dinner to include some of the Dowager's favourite dishes.

Her ladyship, preceded by her maid and assisted by a footman, alighted from the carriage and paused for a moment, looking about her with narrowed eyes, absorbing the fact that her arrival had not, after all, flung the household into the expected consternation and confusion. Then Sir Greydon, with Vivyan at his heels, emerged and came down the steps to welcome her.

It might have been supposed that two such grandsons were a sight to gladden any old lady's heart, but gladness was not the most evident expression in the Dowager's face as she watched them approach. When Greydon bent dutifully to kiss her hand, and said that he was delighted to see her, she replied shortly:

'Easy enough to say, and your manners are always excellent, even if your behaviour is not.' She transferred her attention to Vivyan. 'I understood that *you* were at Newmarket.'

'Came back yesterday, ma'am,' he answered, kissing her hand in his turn and only realizing the imprudence of the admission when she said grimly:

'So that's it! I have you to thank for announcing my approach. I suppose you have been springing your horses all the way from London to be beforehand with the news.'

'Let me take you indoors, ma'am,' Greydon put in soothingly. 'You are tired from the journey, and should not be standing in this hot sunshine.'

'It is no thanks to you, sir, that I am not prostrate from exhaustion,' she informed him testily. 'It would not have been my choice, let me tell you, to make the journey from London during the hottest weather we have had this summer.'

She then allowed them to escort her in to the house, but when Greydon would have led her to one of the saloons, said testily that she would go instead to her own apartments, which no doubt (with another darkling glance at Vivyan) had been made ready for her. She needed to repose herself before dinner.

'But before that, I will see *you*, Greydon, in my drawing-room. Present yourself at six o'clock. Now take me upstairs.'

He did so, with a rueful grin at Vivyan, who, finding himself ignored, beat a hasty and thankful retreat to the library. He was fond of his grandmother, but when she was in this sort of mood he went in considerable dread of her sharp tongue. Grey, he thought, was in for a rare trimming from the old lady.

Sir Greydon himself was of the same opinion, and though he did not find the prospect alarming, as Vivyan would have done, he was conscious of very uncharitable feelings towards Mrs Elverbury, whose interference had done nothing to ease a difficult situation. His grandmother, he knew, would not at first take kindly to his choice of bride; it had been his intention to make the Mallory family known to her, so that she and Dione could become acquainted and, as he was confident they would, friends, before informing her ladyship that this was his future wife. Now he had no choice but to put her immediately in possession of the facts, including the unpalatable one that he had not yet succeeded in persuading Dione to accept him.

On the stroke of six he entered her ladyship's drawing-room, immaculate in the long-tailed coat, knee-breeches and silk stockings which she was old-fashioned enough to consider the only suitable evening wear for a gentleman. His grandmother was seated by the window which looked out over the Italian garden with its statues and formal flowerbeds, flooded now with golden evening light, and he saw with relief (for in spite of her testiness she had looked exceedingly fatigued on her arrival) that her face was less pinched and drawn, and that since she now wore an evening gown she obviously felt well enough to join him and Vivyan at dinner.

'Come now, this is much better,' he said, taking her hand and smiling affectionally down at her. 'I do not like to see you looking as tired as you did when you arrived here.'

'Do not imagine,' she retorted sharply, 'that you can fob me off with these caressing ways. I want an explanation, Greydon, and I want it immediately.'

'An explanation of what, ma'am?'

'Of whatever is going on here. Of your extraordinary behaviour in leaving London at a moment's notice, at the height of the Season, when you had I know not how many engagements. Of suddenly abandoning your courtship of Miss Marstow, just when I was quite convinced that you were on the point of making her an offer—!'

'You convinced yourself of that, ma'am. I did not, for I had no such intention.!'

'It is small wonder,' the Dowager. said bitterly,

gesturing to him to be seated, 'that you are looked upon as a dangerous flirt. Careful mothers are warning their girls against taking seriously any attentions you pay them. Yes, you may laugh, but I am inclined to agree with them.' Her eyes narrowed, and she switched disconcertingly to another matter. 'What brought you to Rushbourne at this time of the year?'

'As I told you, Grandmama, a matter of business.'

'Business!' she repeated with the utmost scorn. 'You have an agent to deal with that.'

'As I am sure you have informed yourself, ma'am, it was Mayhew who brought the matter to my attention. He did not feel qualified to deal with it.' He saw that she still looked disbelieving, and decided that it would be prudent to disclose at least some of the facts. 'To tell you the truth, it concerns Oliver.'

'Oliver?' She stared at him. 'What scrape is he in now?'

'It would appear,' Greydon said carefully, 'that he has absconded to evade his creditors. He was in deep water—deeper, I fancy, than ever before, for he had fallen into the clutches of a cent-per-cent. Not an accredited money-lender, but a back-alley rogue no better than a criminal. I have reason to believe that when Oliver failed to settle, this scoundrel or his henchmen threatened him with violence, and he took fright. At all events, he made off and has not been heard of since.'

'Good riddance!' her ladyship said heartlessly. 'Something of the kind was bound to happen eventually, and if he has involved us in no worse scandal than this, we may be thankful. I always maintained, and I always will, that your grandfather was mistaken in his handling of that affair. Oliver should have been fostered by some respectable family, taught a trade or profession and assisted to make his own way in the world. He should *not* have been reared at Rushbourne, in circumstances which were bound to bring out all his worst characteristics.'

'I heartily agree. With the kindest intentions, Grandfather served Oliver the worst possible turn. I should mention, by the by, that only Mayhew knows that he has gone. Oliver told the other servants that he would be away for a few days, and though by now they must suspect the truth, nothing has yet been said.'

She nodded. 'Very proper. Let us hope that he never returns to plague us again! Well, sir, that expains why you left London, but you could have settled Oliver's affair and been back in town within a week.' She paused inquiringly, but when he made no reply added sharply: 'Who is this young woman with whom you appear to have become entangled?'

'Vivyan tells me,' Greydon said ironically, 'that I am indebted to Mrs Elverbury for noising my affairs abroad, so I feel quite certain you are well aware that the lady you speak of is a relative of old Jonathan Mallory. Her little brother, Theodore, inherited Garth House, and the family have come to make their home there.'

'Very odd people they must be, to take up residence in a house which, by all accounts, is likely to fall into ruins about their ears!'

'Not odd, ma'am. Merely poor,' he replied with a smile. 'Mrs Mallory is the widow of a naval officer.'

'Shabby genteel, I suppose,' her ladyship said scornfully. 'That is all very well, but what I do not understand is why *you* have chosen to interest yourself in such people, beyond the demands of common civility. According to Harriet Elverbury—not that I set any great store by what *she* says—you are at Garth House every day, you squire Miss Mallory about the county, you have even been seen taking the boy driving.'

'Mrs Elverbury has indeed been busy!' There was an edge now to Greydon's voice. 'Let me assure you that her information is accurate, though what concern that is of hers—or, for that matter, of anyone except Miss Mallory and myself—I fail to perceive.'

'Don't try to give *me* one of your famous set-downs,' the Dowager warned him tartly. 'No concern of Harriet's, I agree, but you will admit that *I* have some right to be perturbed when you seem bent upon stirring up the kind of scandal I most deplore.'

'Scandal?' he repeated sternly. 'Enlighten me, ma'am, if you please.'

'Don't be a fool, Greydon!' she retorted impatiently. 'I have never before censured your behaviour, nor will I as long as you are content to amuse yourself in London with high-fliers like the one I saw you with at the beginning of the Season. I will not remain silent, however, when you involve yourself, in our own village, with a young woman of respectable family.'

There was a little silence, and then he spoke in a tone of voice she had never heard from him before.

'If anyone but you, ma'am, had dared to say such a thing—!' He left the sentence unfinished, and after another brief pause, during which she had time to recognize and be startled by the depth of his anger, he continued evenly: 'Both you and Mrs Elverbury mistake the situation. I intend to make Miss Mallory my wife.'

Lady Varleigh gasped, stared at him as though questioning whether or not he was in earnest, decided that he was, and then, after another stunned pause, opened the flood-gates of her wrath. She spoke at some length, of designing minxes and masculine folly, of undutiful grandsons, of irresponsibility and of what was due to an ancient name. Greydon heard her in silence, leaning back in his chair with his gaze fixed on the quizzing-glass which he was swinging to and fro at the end of its ribbon, and when at length she paused, said in the same level voice:

'I feel sure that outburst has relieved your feelings, ma'am, and done you a great deal of good, so now let us consider the matter calmly. How can you possibly pass judgement upon a girl you have never met?'

'I do not need to meet her to know that she is no fit bride for a Varleigh of Rushbourne!'

'That is sheer prejudice. You admit that her birth is respectable, while the fact that she has no portion is immaterial, since I am not hanging out for a rich wife.'

'You are the most perverse creature alive!' her ladyship informed him furiously. 'I could understand it better if you had lost your head over a beautiful face, but Harriet says that Miss Mallory's looks are no more than passable.'

'No,' he admitted with a smile, 'she is not beautiful. She would probably tell you herself, as she has already told me, that she is ordinary and unaccomplished and quite ineligible. What she would not tell you is that she is also gallant and courageous, and faces all her considerable difficulties with a dignity and humour which will, I am quite sure, win both your respect and your admiration. I am convinced that had you met her with your judgement unclouded by Mrs Elverbury's malice, you would have taken an instant liking to her.'

The Dowager was nonplussed. She had watched him flirt expertly with ladies of fashion, both débutantes and young matrons, and had regarded, with the tolerance of a less affected generation, the various Cyprians who had enjoyed his protection, but this was something entirely different. She had never before known him to speak of a woman in just that tone of voice, or with such a look in his eyes.

'I do not understand you,' she said querulously. 'There have been at least a dozen girls, any one of whom you could have had for the asking, who would have made you a suitable wife. Priscilla Marstow was only one of them. Yet you choose a young woman with no experience of the world you live in, who has neither looks nor fortune, but only a tribe of brothers and sisters to be provided for.'

'Scarcely a tribe, ma'am,' he replied patiently. 'Two sisters and one brother.'

'More than enough!' she retorted implacably. She was silent for a moment, regarding him with a frown, and then said abruptly: 'Nearly a year ago, Greydon, you made me a promise. I release you from it.'

He shook his head, smiling at her with affectionate understanding. 'My dear Grandmama, that makes no difference. I have always regarded with aversion the sort of marriage made solely for worldly convenience, with no more than lukewarm tolerance upon either side, but if I had not met Dione I would have entered into just such a marriage in order to keep the promise you speak of. But I did meet her, thank God, and whether or not you hold me to that promise makes not the smallest difference in the world. As soon as I can persuade her to accept me, I shall marry her.'

A gleam of hope appeared in the Dowager's eyes. 'So you have not yet offered for her? No, of course you have not, or you would not be foolish enough to speak of *persuading* her!' She gave a snort of derisive laughter. 'Much persuasion she will need, if she is in the difficulties you say she is!'

'You are mistaken, ma'am. It is precisely because of those difficulties that she would not accept my proposal. She fears, you see, that she might be marrying me merely to solve her problems, and for no other reason.'

'Does she, indeed!' snapped his grandmother, with a sudden and bewildering change of ground. 'Matters have come to a pretty pass when a penniless little nobody takes it upon herself to refuse Varleigh of Rushbourne!' She directed a piercing glance at him beneath her brows. 'You must have been unwontedly inept in your handling of her.'

'I trust not,' he replied equably, but clearly with no intention of enlarging upon the matter. 'Grandmama, I wish very much to present Dione to you. Will you oblige me by inviting Mrs Mallory and her two elder daughters to visit you?'

'I suppose I have no choice,' she replied grudgingly, 'for I shall have to make the girl's acquaintance if you are determined upon this folly. I am well aware that *I* have nothing to say to the matter! You are old enough, one would suppose, to know your own mind—though I place very little dependence upon any man's common sense where a woman is concerned.'

He accepted this meekly, though with a gleam of affectionate amusement in his eyes, saying in a soothing tone: 'You may, however, depend upon my being sufficiently conscious of my duty *not* to make an unsuitable marriage. Dione is poor. That is the only objection which you can in justice offer against her, but she *will* need your help and guidance in a world of which, as you truly observe, she knows very little. I would like to believe that she will receive it.'

'Well, you may believe it!' she snapped. 'I cannot like this marriage, but you should know me better than to imagine I will give the tattle-mongers any chance to say that it has caused a breach between us, or that your wife is not acceptable to your family.'

'Thank you,' he said, taking her hand and kissing it, 'and you *will* like her, you know! Mrs Mallory and Miss Cecilia may exasperate you, for they are both the helpless clinging sort of female I know you find irritating, but Dione is very different, I promise you.'

'Dione!' she repeated querulously. 'Of all the outlandish names to inflict upon a girl—!' Her fingers tightened hard upon his, and she looked up anxiously and searchingly into his face. 'Greydon, are you *certain* she is the right woman for you?'

'Quite certain, my dear,' he replied reassuringly. 'The only woman I have ever met with whom I want to share the rest of my life.'

For a few moments longer she continued to study him, then, as though finally convinced, she nodded resignedly and released his hand, but merely said with all her usual acerbity:

'Then you had better lose no time about it. I want to see an heir to Rushbourne before I die!'

He laughed. 'Grandmama, you are quite outrageous! Where, pray, is your delicacy of mind?'

'Never had any,' she retorted. 'It wasn't fashionable when I was a girl. This generation is a deal too mealy-mouthed!' She looked sharply at him. 'Afraid I will shock this *Dione* of yours?'

He shook his head, quizzing her. 'Not in the least! You will not find her at all missish. As for her name, the rest of her family call her "Dee", and I am sure she will have no objection if you choose to do the same.'

* * *

For the remainder of that day the Mallory family found Dione deeply abstracted, but the younger members supposed this to be the lingering effect of her accident, Cecilia asking her frequently and solicitously if her headache was very bad, until discouraged from doing so by her mother, Mrs Mallory might suspect that her eldest daughter's preoccupation had some other cause, but she kept her own counsel, and merely suggested mildly that it might be a good thing if Dee went early to bed.

Dione agreed with unusual docility, and went up to her room soon after dinner. She had little expectation of the good night's sleep which her mother had confidently predicted would make her feel much more the thing, but she wanted more than anything to be alone to consider, without interruption or distraction, the new and astonishing problem which had been set before her, and upon which a decision must soon be made.

For a little while after she had climbed into bed, drawing the musty curtains to shut out the lingering daylight, she lay in a warm cocoon of darkness and allowed herself the luxury of pretending that she had accepted Sir Greydon's proposal. She was honest enough to admit that she would like nothing better; she had never met anyone with whom she had felt so instantly and completely in sympathy, while the prospect of a future free of financial worries yet with a congenial partner was almost beyond her power to imagine. To be the cherished wife of Greydon Varleigh—could any woman, she wondered, ask for more?

Before long, however, the more practical side of her nature reasserted itself, reminding her that such a future would present difficulties to match its advantages. Sir Greydon's wife would be the mistress of a great house and a great estate, as well as a London mansion where she would be expected to entertain the most brilliant and aristocratic company, and how would plain Dione Mallory fare then? To be sure, she could depend upon her husband's support, but she would need, too, the help and encouragement of his family, and particularly of old

Lady Varleigh, if she were to avoid the many pitfalls which would lie in wait, and what right had she to expect that she would receive it?

Yet there was her own family to consider. Ought she not, for their sake, seize the glittering opportunity offered to her, and secure their future as well as her own? The world would not blame her for doing so; it might even regard it as her duty, and consider her extraordinarily fortunate to find duty and inclination going hand-in-hand. Perhaps she was creating difficulties where none existed. For the family's sake she had contemplated marrying Eustace Winton even though she did not like him; why hesitate to accept Sir Greydon because she liked him so much?

This, Dione realized suddenly, brought her to the heart of the matter, and face to face with the only question of any real significance, since if it could be honestly answered it would dispose of all the rest. She liked Greydon immensely, but did she love him? She simply did not know. There had been no romantic interludes in her life; no girlish infatuations, no young men swearing undying devotion and begging her to marry them; even Eustace, although he had proposed many times, had never once said that he loved her, or addressed to her even the mildest endearment. She had no yardstick whatsoever by which to measure the depth of her feeling for Sir Greydon. Only a deep, instinctive conviction that to marry him she must be able to offer him a love as profound as that he professed for her; and a certainty that to lose his companionship and support would be a desolation beyond bearing.

She fell asleep with her dilemma still unresolved, and awoke with her mind in the same turmoil of uncertainty. She wondered whether Greydon would come to Garth House that day, and did not know whether she hoped that he would, or feared it. One thing at least, she thought with exasperation, could not be denied. His declaration had turned her whole world upside down, and robbed her of all her usual ability to come to a decision; she did not even know whether she was happy or wretched.

In an attempt to divert her mind from the questions teasing it, she flung herself energetically into household tasks, so energetically, in fact, that by early afternoon she had nothing left to do. It was another hot day, and Mrs Mallory, her sewing in her lap, was dozing gently in the parlour. Cecilia, who possessed considerable artistic ability, was giving Edwina a drawing-lesson, and they had carried their sketch-books out into the garden. Theo was off about some mysterious business of his own with Jem Durridge. Dione, looking restlessly about for some task with which to occupy herself, decided to make a start on turning out the stillroom.

This was situated at the back of the house near the kitchen, and looked as though it had not been touched for decades. Its walls were lined with shelves which bore a bewildering collection of jars, bottles and boxes all thickly coated with dust and cobwebs, while the table in the middle of the room was similarly cluttered. Dione, swathed in apron and mob-cap, viewed the chaos with distaste and set briskly to work.

Within half an hour she was regretting her choice of occupation, for the stillroom faced south, and the window, tightly closed for years, now refused to open. Dione was hot, dusty and uncomfortable, and in no mood to welcome her brother when he put his head round the door.

'You had better not come in, Theo,' she warned him sharply. 'It is very dirty, and I am far too busy to attend to you.'

'Yes, but, Dee, listen! We have something to tell you. It's important!' Theodore came farther into the room, revealing, to Dione's indignation, that Jem Durridge was close upon his heels. 'Come on, Jem! My sister is here.'

Jem obeyed rather bashfully, knuckling his forehead to Dione and coming no farther than the threshold. Theodore grabbed him impatiently by the arm and dragged him forward, pushing the door shut behind them and saying eagerly:

'Dee, you know Ibstone says the stables are locked up because the roof is unsafe? Well, that's all a hum! We have just been in there, and there's nothing wrong with the roof at all—at least, no more with any of the other roofs here.'

'Theo, I have no time for any of your hoaxes. The stable door is still padlocked.'

'Yes, but Jem said that if we could get into the loft we could see if it was safe, and if it was we could get down into the stables. So we climbed on to the roof of the coach-house—!'

'You did what?' Dione was horrified. 'Merciful Heaven, you might both have been killed! Jem, it was very wrong of you to suggest such a prank. I am exceedingly angry with you.'

'Oh, Dee, stop fussing and listen!' Theodore implored her. 'We got into the loft through that little window at the end, and what do you think? We could hear a horse moving about down below.'

Dione regarded him exasperatedly. 'Another ghost, no doubt! Theo, I warned you!'

'No, no! It was a real horse, in the stall right at the far end. A prime bit of blood-and-bone, too, but the oddest thing of all is that Jem recognized it.' He prodded his friend in the ribs, adding generously: 'Go on, Jem! Tell her!'

'It be that big grey o' Mr Varleigh's, miss,' Jem blurted scarlet-faced. 'A nasty-tempered brute it be, so I wouldn't let Master Theo near it.' He saw that Miss Mallory was staring unbelievingly at him, and added desperately: 'That be gospel-truth, miss! Anyone in the village will tell you the same.'

Dione felt for the edge of the table and leaned against it for support, her thoughts racing. There was no reason to doubt what the boys were saying, or to suppose that Jem was mistaken, so their discovery could mean only one thing. Jack Ibstone—or, more probably, his whole family—were in league with Oliver Varleigh. They had been concealing his horse at Garth House; and if the horse, why not Varleigh himself? That would explain his complete and baffling disappearance.

Excitement was rising in her, and the thought that here, at last, was an opportunity to do something for

Greydon. There was no time yet to consider all the implications of the discovery, but two facts were crystal-clear. Greydon himself must be summoned without delay, and the two boys prevented from speaking of the matter to anyone else.

'Are you quite sure about the horse, Jem?' she asked, and he nodded.

'Certain sure, miss. It be Mr Varleigh's grey, right enough!'

'Mr Varleigh is Sir Greydon's cousin, Dee,' Theodore put in helpfully. 'He used to live at the Abbey.'

'Yes, Theo, I know.' Dione stopped short, frowning at him. 'Why do you say "used to live at the Abbey"?'

He came closer, lowering his voice to a thrilling whisper. 'Because he has disappeared. Dee, we think Ibstone has murdered him.'

'Theo!' Dione was shocked. 'You should not say such a thing, even as a joke.'

'I wasn't joking!' he replied indignantly. 'Only think, Dee! Mr Varleigh *has* disappeared—Jem says everyone in the village knows that. He said he was going away for a few days, and he rode off on his horse and hasn't been seen since. That was weeks ago, and now his horse is hidden in our stables. So where can Mr Varleigh be?'

Where, indeed? Jem was nodding solemn agreement, and it occurred to Dione that to stamp too firmly on their gruesome theory would be to invite the two boys to speculate upon the only likely alternative. She said hastily:

'Well, wherever he is, and whatever the reason for his horse being concealed here, one thing at least is plain to me. Sir Greydon would be exceedingly angry if we noised abroad this very odd affair before informing him of it. He must be told immediately. Jem, if I write him a note, will you carry it to the Abbey?'

He assented eagerly, and Dione, warning them to remain where they were until she returned, hurried to the parlour for pen and paper. Mrs Mallory, rousing with a start, regarded her with astonishment and some dismay.

'Dee, what in the world have you been doing?'

'I have begun to clean the stillroom, Mama. It is in a shocking state.'

'So are you, my love,' her mother informed her frankly. 'For pity's sake, go and take off that horrid cap and apron, and wash your face. You look like a scullery-maid.'

'Yes, Mama. I will do so directly,' Dione replied absently, sitting down at the table and dipping her pen in the ink. 'I have to write this first.'

Mrs Mallory continued to hold forth rather fretfully on the impropriety of a lady, however indigent, undertaking tasks which should only be performed by a servant, but Dione, intent upon conveying to Greydon the maximum amount of information in the minimum number of words, paid no heed to the gently querulous monologue. On the contrary, she welcomed it, since Mrs Mallory's preoccupation with her daughter's shocking appearance prevented her from speculating upon the letter Dione was writing.

When she returned to the stillroom she found the boys happily discussing the probable whereabouts of Oliver Varleigh's body, and gathered that while Jem favoured the notion of a hiding-place in Garth Wood, Theodore was of the opinion that to dig a grave in the vegetable garden would have occasioned less remark.

'Horrid boy!' Dione observed dispassionately, overhearing this. 'Do you wish me never to eat vegetables again? Here is the note, Jem. Go as quickly as you can, and make sure that they know at the Abbey that the message is urgent. It will be best if you do not part with it to anyone but Sir Greydon himself, if that is possible.'

He assured her that he understood, and hurried away, while Theodore, his request to be allowed to accompany him unhesitatingly refused by his sister, scowled sulkily for a little while but found the possibilities of the situation too exciting not to be discussed.

'What do you suppose Sir Greydon will do?' he asked, watching Dione clear the last of the clutter from the table. 'Will he send for the Constable and have Ibstone dragged off to prison? Will they dig up the vegetable garden?'

'Neither, I imagine,' she replied dampingly. 'What a little ghoul you are, Theo! I expect Sir Greydon will simply question Ibstone about the horse, and ask him if he knows what has become of Mr Varleigh—if he has indeed disappeared. It is quite likely, you know, that he went off somewhere by Mail coach, and has already written to Sir Greydon to tell him where he has gone, and why.'

'If he has, it will be the shabbiest thing!' Theodore declared hotly. 'And even if he has, why should his horse be hidden in our stables? There must be some mystery about that at all events.'

'Perhaps there is, but that is Sir Greydon's business and not ours. Now mind, Theo! When he comes, I will have no impertinent questions or suggestions put to him about this matter. In fact, unless he gives you leave, you will not breathe a word on that, if you please.'

He did so, but looked so crestfallen that she relented a little, and assured him that since it was he and Jem who had uncovered the mystery, no doubt Sir Greydon would tell them as much about it as was good for them to know.

'And that is all I can promise you,' she added with finality. 'Now pray go and occupy yourself somewhere—but *not* in the neighbourhood of the stables.'

'I shall go and wait for Sir Greydon,' he decided. 'If I sit by the pool I shall see him as soon as he arrives.'

'Very well, but you are likely to wait for some time. It will take Jem at least half an hour to reach the Abbey, and even he may not find Sir Greydon at home.'

The prospect did not appear to worry Theodore, and he went cheerfully away to take up his self-appointed vigil, leaving his sister free at last to consider all the aspects of this totally unexpected development. She had no doubt at all that Oliver Varleigh was concealed somewhere in that part of Garth House where the Ibstones' had their quarters, rooms into which Dione herself had never intruded. He must have been established there even before the Mallory family arrived, which would account for their hostile reception; and yet their arrival had not been unexpected. Even if some unsuspected bond existed between Oliver Varleigh and the Ibstones, and he had planned to lie low at Garth House after the theft of the Medallion, why had he not left as soon as Mrs Ibstone received Dione's letter informing her that they were coming?

Sitting with her elbows on the table and her chin on her hands, Dione pondered that question, until suddenly she recalled their first night in the house, and Theodore's insistence that he heard voices, and a tapping sound. A sound which, later, he had identified as that of someone lame walking with a stick. When he played his prank with the walking-stick he had found, Molly had been horrified; not, as they supposed, by superstitious dread of Jonathan Mallory's ghost, but because she feared that the secret occupant of the house had betrayed himself. Oliver Varleigh had not originally planned to hide at Garth House. Some accident must have befallen him, and he had sought refuge here because he was unable to make his escape; and since he was still here, surely the Varleigh Medallion must be here also? Even if it were concealed somewhere, Dione had no doubt that Greydon would know how to compel his cousin to disclose its hiding-place.

The thought of Greydon, and his possibly imminent arrival, made Dione recollect her present appearance. She started up in dismay and, closing the door upon the grimy disorder of the stillroom, hurried up to her bedchamber, where she washed, and put on a fresh muslin gown. She had tidied her hair, and was just placing a handkerchief in her reticule when a faint sound reached her from the corridor outside the room. No tapping stick this time; just a stealthy, uneven footstep approaching the door of the Great Bedchamber.

* * *

For a moment of horrified stillness. Dione stood petrified, and then, as the latch began to lift, instinct sent her flitting on tiptoe through the open door into Theodore's room. Pushing the door nearly shut she stood motionless, almost afraid to breathe, peering through the crack at the tiny portion of her own room still visible to her. She heard the door softly open and close, the limping footfall drew nearer and a man crossed her line of vision.

Dione's eyes widened with astonishment, for this was not the first time she had seen him. Moderately tall and slightly stooping, hair so fair that it looked almost white—save that he was booted and wearing a long, caped overcoat, this was the figure she had glimpsed by mistly moonlight in the same room two nights before.

He had passed out of sight in the direction of the fireplace, but she could still hear the sound of furtive movement. The seconds dragged by, and then at last he reappeared, limping towards the door; he was withdrawing his hand from the pocket of his coat, and that side of the garment was now dragged out of shape by the weight of some heavy object. In the light of what she already knew, the meaning of the incident was plain. Oliver Varleigh was recovering the proceeds of his crime, prior to making his escape.

It could not be mere coincidence that he should do so at this precise moment. Perhaps, from a window, he had seen the boys climbing into or out of the stable-loft; perhaps one of the Ibstones had overheard them talking to Dione in the stillroom; the reason was unimportant. What mattered was to prevent his departure, for somehow he must be detained until Greydon arrived.

With not the smallest notion of how this was to be accomplished, she stole across the Great Bedchamber, listened at the door, and then peeped out to find the corridor deserted. Of course, he would have used the backstairs. Dione waited a few moments to give him time to reach the bottom, and then went quietly down them herself.

This brought her to the stone-flagged passage on to which the various domestic offices opened, and which ended at a door giving on to the stableyard. It was deserted, but a murmur of voices came from behind the closed door of the kitchen. Pausing outside, she was able to distinguish what was being said.

The first voice she heard was Molly's, sharp with anxiety and dismay. 'They'll catch you for sure! You haven't sat a horse this month past, and your leg be'ant strong enough yet for a long, hard ride. Suppose that nasty brute was to throw you again?'

'He might at that,' Ibstone's surly tones broke in. 'A sight too fresh, he be, having been cooped up all this time wi' next to no chance to stretch his legs. 'Twere as much as I could do to saddle him and lead him out, and I'd no more have ventured to throw a leg across him than I'd try to fly.'

'Confound you, Jack, stop croaking!' A voice now that Dione had never heard before. 'Do you think I mean to stay here to be thrown into gaol for debt—for if you think my precious cousin will lift a finger to help me you're fair and far out!'

'But he would, Oliver! You know as he would!' Molly sounded tearful now. 'Think o' the talk there'd be if you was prisoned! Sir Greydon'd never stand for that, nor would her ladyship. Too proud by half!'

'You're right there, by God!' Varleigh agreed savagely. 'I've had to suffer their damned pride all my life, and I've had my fill of it. Do you think I would ever be allowed to forget this affair, even if Greydon settled my debts? I'd rather take my chance on getting out of the country.'

'There's money needed for a journey of that sort.' Mrs Ibstone spoke for the first time, her flat, practical tone a sharp contrast to Varleigh's voice. 'You'll need to change horses, and there'll be a passage aboard ship to buy as well. How will you manage that with only a guinea or two in your pocket?'

Dione scarcely heeded Varleigh's reply, her mind being occupied by the discovery that the Ibstones were plainly in ignorance of Oliver's possession of the Medallion, and of the money which Greydon said he had stolen at the same time. He must have convinced them that he was merely fleeing from his creditors, which explained his need to recover the stolen valuables himself. She had thought it odd that he should take such a risk when Molly could easily have fetched them to him, but it was plain now that neither Molly nor her parents knew about them. No doubt, on his arrival, Varleigh had been accommodated in the Great Bedchamber, and had seized the first opportunity to conceal there the proceeds of his crime.

Molly was speaking again, imploringly: 'Oh, my dearie, don't go! What if they still be looking for you, them as you owes money to? There's more to fear from them than ever there is from Sir Greydon. He'll pay your debts, for his own sake and his grandma's, if not for yours.'

'I tell you I'll not be beholden to him. Now loose me, Moll, there's a good girl, or I'll not be away before he comes! I'll write to you, I give you my word, as soon as I'm safely out of England.'

A wail from Molly suggested that this promise was small consolation. Above it, Dione heard Ibstone say roughly:

'The lass be right! You'd do better to bide. Besides, what are *we* to say to Sir Greydon when he comes? We've hid you here, for Molly's sake, but I never reckoned it to be known. Like as not we'll be turned out o' house and home on your account.'

'Damn it, man, tell him the brats were lying, playing off a hoax on Miss Mallory! If I'm away, and you have all done your part in getting rid of any trace that I was ever here, there will be only their word that my horse was ever in the stables. No one else saw the brute there. Now I must go, or we shall all find ourselves in the basket.'

Dione heard Ibstone's reluctant assent, then movement within the room, and knew that she had no choice but to intervene. Drawing a deep breath, she pushed open the door and stepped into the kitchen.

A stunned silence greeted her. Oliver Varleigh, trying to extricate himself from Molly's tearful embrace, stared in ludicrous dismay, an emotion clearly shared by his companions. Dione, advancing into the room, addressed him with a calmness she did not entirely feel.

'I fear that you find yourself already there, Mr Varleigh. It is true that I did not see your horse, but I do see you, and even if you force your way out of the house before Sir Greydon comes, I assure you that he will have no hesitation in accepting *my* word that you were here.' She looked at Mrs Ibstone, realizing the necessity of winning the woman and her husband on to her side. 'It was wrong, and exceedingly foolish of you to hide Mr Varleigh here, but no doubt you did so with the kindest intentions and so I shall not hold it against you.'

The housekeeper's expression did not relax, but Dione saw a flicker of astonishment and relief in her eyes, and knew that she had won an ally; and where Mrs Ibstone led, her husband would undoubtedly follow. Molly had flung herself down by the table and was weeping noisily with her head buried in her arms; clearly she need not be taken into account. There remained only Oliver Varleigh.

'As for you, sir,' Dione continued, turning to him again, 'I must insist that you remain here until Sir Greydon comes. I do not think we shall be obliged to wait for long.'

He had recovered a certain degree of composure by this time, and studied her with a faintly sneering expression. Seeing him distinctly for the first time, Dione could trace a certain resemblance to the Varleighs in his face, even though his colouring was so different. Clearly he had once been handsome—she thought that as a boy he must have possessed an almost feminine degree of good looks—but his features now were marked by lines of discontent and self-indulgence. He said ironically:

'And if I do not choose to wait, ma'am, do you imagine that you can compel me to do so?'

He stared at her from narrowed eyes, clearly wondering how much she knew, and Dione looked steadily back, silently asking herself whether, if it came to the point, Ibstone would obey a command to detain

Varleigh by force. Then, into the tenseness of that pause, came the sound of the door from the stableyard being flung open, and the clatter of Theodore's footsteps as he ran past towards the stillroom. Another door opened and closed, and then he came back more slowly, while Dione, desperately hoping that she had correctly interpreted the reason for his return to the house, raised her voice to call:

'I am here, Theo! In the kitchen.'

The door opened and he came in, saying eagerly: 'Dee, I came to find you. Will you—!' He broke off, staring with widening eyes at Oliver Varleigh, and then raised his voice to a shout. 'Sir Greydon! Sir Greydon, come quickly!'

Hasty footsteps sounded, and Theodore moved aside to let Greydon come past him into the kitchen. He checked just inside the door, his glance going swiftly from Dione to the Ibstones and then to Oliver, who was staring at him in consternation, his face a sickly grey. Satisfaction leapt into Greydon's eyes, but all he said was:

'What a confounded nuisance you are, Oliver! Do you mean to tell me that you have been skulking here for more than a month?'

Oliver did not appear to be capable for the moment of telling him anything. Dione said in an urgent whisper:

'He has the Medallion in his pocket. It was hidden in my room.'

Greydon flashed her a smile. 'You wonderful girl!' he said softly, and extended a compelling hand towards his cousin. 'Come, Oliver, hand it over! You can keep the money you stole, but I want the Medallion.'

'Well, I be damned!' Ibstone exclaimed. 'I thought all along there were more to it than debts.'

No one paid any heed to this interjection. Greydon waited with outstretched hand; Oliver retreated a pace or two until he fetched up with his back against the big, scrubbed table in the middle of the room. His face was livid now, and sweat glistened on his brow.

'Very well, damn you!' he said in a shrill, cracked voice. 'You shall have it!'

He thrust his right hand into his pocket, and a little frown of perplexity creased Dione's brow, but before she could speak the hand emerged again, holding not the Varleigh Medallion but a pistol, which he levelled at Greydon. Molly uttered a stifled scream.

'Thought you held the whip hand, didn't you?' Oliver sneered in the same shrill voice. 'Thought you had only to give an order and I'd obey, as though I were one of your poor damned troopers. Well, you're out there! I know I'm done for, but by God! I'll make you pay for the way you've despised me, you and your old beldame of a grandmother who always hated me. I may be finished, but the accursed Varleighs will be finished, too, and can rot in hell!'

Dione moved softly forward, two quick paces which brought her between Greydon and Oliver, facing the pistol. Greydon made an instinctive, horrified movement, checked even as it began, for Oliver's finger was trembling on the trigger and the muzzle of the weapon was barely a yard from Dione's breast.

'Pray do not be foolish, Mr Varleigh,' she said breathlessly. 'You are by no means "finished", for Sir Greydon, I know, has no intention of punishing you. All he desires is the return of the Medallion.' He stared uncertainly at her, and she added persuasively: 'Come now, put up the pistol! You would have to shoot *me*, you know, and I am persuaded that you wish me no harm.'

For a few seconds longer he continued to stare at her, while the whole room, it seemed, held its breath, and then the hand holding the pistol wavered and sank to his side. Ibstone, who was nearest, grasped his flaccid wrist and twisted the weapon from his grasp, and with a shuddering groan Oliver sank down on the bench by the table and buried his face in his hands.

Dione swayed suddenly and Greydon stepped quickly forward to support her, saying under his breath, in a shaken voice:

'Dione, my darling!'

She was trembling violently, and thankful for a moment to lean against him, but almost at once recovered herself sufficiently to say unsteadily:

'The Medallion—is in his *other* pocket.'

Greydon, becoming aware of the curious eyes about them, put her into the chair which Mrs Ibstone had dragged forward, and then bent to feel in the left pocket of Oliver's coat. When he straightened up again he was holding a great, shining circle of gold ablaze with precious stones.

There was a concerted gasp of amazement. Theodore let his breath go in a long, low whistle of astonishment.

'Is *that* what he had stolen?' he asked incredulously. 'What is it, sir?'

'The Varleigh Medallion, Theo,' Greydon replied, and looked down at Dione with a smile which was for her alone. 'The Varleigh luck!'

* * *

More hasty footsteps sounded in the passage and Mr Calderwood came impetuously into the room, to halt just inside the door to stare with dropped jaw at the scene before him. Greydon said, with a very fair assumption of his usual manner:

'Ah, Vivyan! It is fortunate that you accompanied me, for I have a favour to ask of you. Will you be good enough to take my curricle, drive Oliver to the "Royal George" and make certain that he boards the mail coach for London?' To Oliver he added: 'When you arrive in town, procure a room at Fenton's Hotel and wait there until you hear again from me.'

Mr Varleigh cast him a malevolent glance. 'Curse you! I don't take orders from you.'

'I am sure that you will, for the alternative is so very unpleasant. I should perhaps inform you that an officer of the law is at present putting up at the inn in Brambledon.'

'Devil take your officer of the law!' Varleigh was rapidly recovering his effrontery, and spoke with a sneer. 'Don't try to gull me into believing you would hand me over to him, and have the precious Varleigh name dragged through the courts!'

'Grey!' Vivyan had been staring at Oliver with

gathering wrath, and now spoke in a tone of ferocious longing. 'Let me take him out into the yard and teach him a lesson. *You* may not feel inclined to soil your hands on him, but I'm not so particular.'

'I believe neither of us need put ourselves to that trouble, Vivyan,' Greydon said contemptuously. 'Remember, Oliver, that it is not only the Runners who have been searching for you. There are some very ugly customers indeed who are eager to have a word with you about a loan which has not been repaid, and if you decline to do as I say, I shall have no choice but to hand you over to them. On the whole, I believe you will do better to accept what I offer.'

From the alteration in Mr Varleigh's demeanour caused by this threat it was plain that he believed it, too. Greydon nodded to Vivyan, who grasped the older man by the arm and hauled him, unresisting, to his feet. To Oliver, Greydon added curtly:

'I will arrange a passage to America, and your allowance will continue to be paid to you as long as you make no attempt to return to England.'

Oliver Varleigh raised his head and looked at his kinsman with an expression of concentrated venom in his livid face.

'Go to hell!' he said viciously, and allowed Vivyan to thrust him before him out of the room.

Sir Greydon looked sternly at the Ibstones, who were watching him apprehensively. Mrs Ibstone hurried into speech.

'We never knew, sir! He told us he was on the run from his creditors. His horse had throwed him and hurt his leg so he couldn't ride, and he begged us to hide him here until he was well. We never meant no harm!'

'You betrayed the trust reposed in you,' Greydon said coldly. 'If the decision were mine, you would all be turned off without a reference, but you are not in my service and I have no authority to punish you. It must be for Miss Mallory to decide.' He looked at Dione, noting with relief that though she was still very pale, she appeared to have recovered her composure. 'Well, ma'am?'

'Oh, miss, please don't turn us off!' Mrs Ibstone's belligerence had totally deserted her. Her usually florid face was pale, and her numerous chins wobbled to the tearful quivering of her lips. 'There didn't seem no harm in it! We'd known Mr Oliver all his life—him and Jack was cronies when they was lads—and there was Molly begging and pleading with me to take him in. They—I know I shouldn't speak of such to a young lady and you'll maybe not take my meaning—but her and Mr Oliver—!'

'Pray do not go on, Mrs Ibstone. I understand perfectly what you mean,' Dione replied with dignity, taking care not to catch Greydon's eye. 'I think it exceedingly foolish of her, and wrong in you to permit it, but that is neither here nor there. Since you did not know that Mr Varleigh had robbed Sir Greydon—!'

'That we didn't miss! He'd have been sent packing if I had known, for thieving I don't hold with, and never will!'

'It is true that they did not know,' Dione said to Greydon. 'I discovered that from what I heard said in this room before I came in. Do you not think that if they all swear to keep the whole matter secret, no more need to be said?'

'If that is what you wish.' He turned to the Ibstones. 'Are you prepared to make—and keep—such a promise?'

He was fervently assured that they were, and three separate undertakings were promptly given, even Molly, roughly shaken by her mother, lifting a tear-swollen face long enough to swear that no word of the affair would ever pass her lips. Dione then turned her attention to Theodore, and to Jem, who had sidled in to join his friend just after Mr Calderwood's departure, and had since been regaled, in an excited undertone, with an account of all that had happened.

'You must both give your word, too,' she said gravely, 'for there would be dreadful consequences if a single word of what happened here today was ever breathed outside these walls. It is a secret which we must all guard with our lives.'

This was exactly the right tone to take with two small boys with a thirst for adventure, and the required promises were earnestly and enthusiastically given. Since they would have the satisfaction of discussing the matter endlessly between themselves, both Dione and Greydon had every confidence that these would be kept, and had no hesitation in allowing the boys to take themselves off.

When they had gone, Greydon offered Dione his arm. 'I think,' he remarked, 'that it will be advisable for us to go out through the stableyard and into the gardens, for it would present a very odd appearance if your mother or sister chanced to see us coming from this part of the house.'

She agreed, remarking as they went across the yard: 'What a mercy you arrived when you did! I had no expectation of seeing you so soon, and was at my wits' end to know how to prevent Mr Varleigh from leaving the house.'

'I was already on my way here,' he explained. 'When the Runner reported to me today, he told me that he had just learned of an association between my cousin and Molly Ibstone. That in itself seemed of little significance, but combined with the odd occurrences you had described to me, I felt that it merited further investigation, and Vivyan and I were driving to call upon you when we encountered young Durridge hurrying towards Rushbourne with your note. We took him up with us, and when we reached here Theo met me and told me that you were in the stillroom. Since we wished to investigate the stables, and I had no wish to alarm your mother and sisters, it seemed best to drive straight into the yard and send him to fetch you.'

They continued to discuss the day's events as they went out of the yard and along the path, but instead of going towards the house, Greydon led her firmly into the rose-garden.

'Now,' he said, halting and turning to face her, 'we are sufficiently private for me to take you to task for giving me the worst, most terrifying moment of my life. Dione, how could you even *think* of doing anything as crazy, as foolhardy, as placing yourself in front of a cocked and loaded pistol?'

Her gaze, which had lifted inquiringly to meet his, dropped again. She said in a low voice: 'I did not even stop to think. I did not need to. He meant to kill you. Just for that moment he truly intended to do it. I had to try to bring him to his senses.'

There was a little silence. A bee buzzed between them, and a breath of wind sent a shower of rose petals fluttering and drifting about them.

'Yesterday,' Greydon said quietly at length, 'I asked you a question which you did not feel able to answer. Can you answer it now?' When she did not reply, or look at him, he took her face gently between his hands and turned it towards him. 'Dione, not half an hour ago you risked your life because mine was in danger. Surely now I have a right to hope that you feel more for me than friendship?'

'Yes.' She stood, unresisting, meeting his eyes steadily now although colour had risen in her cheeks. 'I do love you, Greydon, but that does not alter the fact that our stations in life—!'

'It alters everything,' he said decisively, and swept her into his arms. 'I warned you, did I not, that next time I proposed to you it would not be in a curricle? Permit me to demonstrate why.' He kissed her, with such thoroughness that when finally released she was too breathless for protest or argument. 'Dione, my gallant, precious love, will you marry me?'

She nodded meekly, drawing a long breath of sheer happiness. 'Yes, because at last I am so sure it will be for the right reason that I would marry you even if you were as poor as I am myself.' She gave a quiet chuckle as he uttered a stifled sound and buried his face against her hair. '*Now* what have I said to make you laugh . . . ?'

A SPEAKING LIKENESS (A Georgian Romance)
BY SHEILA BISHOP

Diana Pentland, a young widow, could hardly avoid befriending the miserable, unwed girl she found on her doorstep. But when the girl refused to divulge her name, nor that of her seducer—and then disappeared, leaving behind her new-born son—Diana almost regretted her charity. An attorney persuaded her to adopt the boy, and in return an anonymous client would provide for them generously. Soon she came to love little 'Hop' as her own.

His identity and that of the mysterious benefactor remained secret, until a chance visit to Brandham Castle, when Hop's incredible likeness to the heir led Diana to believe she had solved the mystery. As she found herself drawn deeper into the family secrets, she also found protection and love from a very unexpected source.

0 552 10659 3 60p

BLOSSOM LIKE A ROSE
BY NORAH LOFTS

Philip Ollenshaw was the eldest son of Sir John Ollenshaw, and heir to the Manor of Marshalsea. But there his advantages ended, for Philip was a cripple—shy, sensitive, nervous—and in his father he aroused only hatred and contempt.

But Philip, physically a lesser man than his father, had courage and vision. When he fell in love with Linda Seabrook he renounced his inheritance and joined a band of colonists bound for America, committing himself to a life of hardship and endeavour.

And, carving out a future from the wilderness, surviving the perils of Indian raids and the harshness of life under Puritan rule, Philip found his strength was the abiding force of the community...

0 552 10726 3 85p